MW00398580

MARCUS

MICHAEL EDWARD GIESLER

MARCUS

A NOVEL

Depicting the lives of the early Christians in Rome

 Scepter

© 2004, 2006 Michael Edward Giesler

Published by Scepter Publishers, Inc.

www.scepterpublishers.org
All rights reserved

ISBN-13: 978-1-59417-018-8
ISBN-10: 1-59417-018-5

FIRST PRINTING 2004
SECOND PRINTING (REVISED) 2006
THIRD PRINTING 2009
FOURTH PRINTING 2011

Text composed in Adobe Caslon fonts

Printed in the United States of America

Contents

*To Saints Paul, Justin Martyr, and
Josemaría Escrivá—may their message and spirit
be found in these pages*

PRELUDE

A Synopsis of *Junia*

Junia, the very talented and attractive daughter of Gaius Metellus Cimber, Senator of Rome, has a dear friend, Marcia, who has been exceptionally kind to her on many occasions—including a hard illness. She also has a brother, Marcus, four years older than she, and a philosophy student. Her mother, Aurelia, is very much a socialite. While waiting for Marcia to visit her at the family's country villa, Junia suddenly and unexpectedly discovers that Marcia and her father, Diodorus, were Christians, and that they have been executed in the arena. This news depresses and confuses her tremendously.

On returning to Rome, Junia receives a mysterious letter delivered by Scintilla, a former servant of Diodorus's household, a letter written by Marcia before her death. In it, Marcia expresses her love for Jesus Christ and her desire that Junia somehow get to know him. After reading the letter, Junia, despite the risk, decides to visit the catacomb where Marcia is buried. There she meets Scintilla again. After praying at Marcia's tomb and seeing a fresco of Christ the Good Shepherd on the catacomb wall, she becomes interested in Christianity and asks Scintilla to come to her home to teach her about the Christ and his Way. In the catacomb she also meets the Christian family of Justus and Constantia, who take her back home in their fish cart.

As Scintilla teaches her about Christ and his Way, Junia finds herself loving him, and quite soon decides to take the tremendous risk of becoming a Christian. During this time, she is engaged to be married to Quintus, a young and promising member of the Praetorian Guard, who has distinguished himself in military service. In the meantime,

Agrippina, a friend of Junia's mother, and her daughter Livia plot against Junia out of jealousy, not only because of her talent and beauty, but because of her engagement to Quintus, who Livia had hoped would marry her. Junia receives Baptism, Confirmation, and Holy Communion in the same catacomb where Marcia was buried, and she experiences great joy and fulfillment. As she leaves the catacomb, however, she is recognized by a spy sent by Agrippina and Livia to keep track of her movements.

In her first weeks as a Christian, she prays especially for her family, and tries to help her brother, Marcus, understand the teachings of Christianity, but without success. She also helps take care of the very sick father of Cynthia, her servant; and her undertaking to act as nurse to a slave soon becomes widespread news in Rome. Livia's father, Antonius, tries to blackmail Gaius Metellus by means of the spy's testimony about seeing Junia in the catacomb, but this testimony is rejected for lack of juridical validity. Within a very short time, however, mostly because of rumors spread by Agrippina and Livia in Rome, Junia is widely suspected of being a Christian and is asked by the Emperor and her father to take the anti-Christian oath required by law, and to offer wine and incense to the Emperor's statue. Junia refuses, despite very strong and persistent pressure from her family and a moving letter from Quintus, her fiancé. In the meantime, she is able to give some first ideas about Christianity to Cynthia, who has become open to Christ's message through Junia's repeated kindnesses to her.

Junia is sentenced to be decapitated in the Colosseum. Conquering her fears and doubts by recognizing God as her loving Father, and remembering the Good Shepherd and his cross, she accepts her death sentence with supernatural faith and courage—even with good humor. As she is being led into the arena, she gives Cynthia a small scroll with a wax seal: it is the same letter that Marcia had written to her the year before.

AWAKENING

I.

Marcus did not wish to go to Junia's execution, nor even to see her as she was being led down the street in the chariot. He tried to bury himself in a Stoic treatise about suffering and resignation that his father gave him to read, seeking to overcome his strong emotion at his sister's death. But he could not concentrate. He could not grasp how she could have given up everything, her future, her reputation, her very life—for a man who had died a hundred years before in a distant land. He had not thought highly of her friend Marcia. She had seemed rather silly and frivolous to him, though there was a strength in her that he could not understand.

The weeks after Junia's death saw some changes at the home of Gaius, on the Esquiline Hill. Cynthia had been discharged, for there was no longer a need for her to stay. Marcus, for one, would miss her; he had always admired her level-headedness, and she knew her place as a slave. She left Gaius's home just a few days after the execution, and Marcus didn't know where she went. He assumed that his father had sold her to another household in Rome, to be the maid-servant of another young woman of Junia's rank in society.

Marcus missed having conversations with his sister. She had a remarkably good mind and could grasp concepts and questions that he brought from his classes with Strabo at the Athenaeum.* But, in his opinion, she had an irrational

---

* The Athenaeum was established by Emperor Hadrian c. A.D. 130 as a center for lectures and readings by well-known teachers of rhetoric and philosophy. These lectures attracted many students, although the more famous such academies were found in the eastern part of the Empire—Athens, Alexandria (Egypt), Ephesus, and Antioch (Syria).

streak in her when it came to Christianity. He remembered his last conversation with her, when he tried to convince her to take the anti-Christian oath and offer incense to the Emperor's statue. He encouraged her to say the words of the oath but to bless Christ in her heart as she said them. Junia had shot back: "And would you do that to your best friend?" Those words stayed with him, for he was vaguely aware that he never had had a best friend.

He had many acquaintances, several intelligent and witty classmates, both from Rome and parts of the Empire . . . but he never had a close friend. He remembered Aristotle's famous criticism of his teacher Plato: *Plato is my friend, but truth is more my friend.* That thought consoled him somewhat, for he did consider himself to be committed to the truth. He had even risked his father's disfavor by attending philosophy lectures, instead of going into rhetoric and oratory. Philosophy was the reason why he had rejected Christianity; it was irrational to him that people could rise from the dead, or that an all-powerful God would allow himself to be crucified. Junia's arguments had not convinced him.

It was not long before he was attending lectures again at the Athenaeum. With the help of one of his teachers he was doing a study of the differences between Heraclitus and Parmenides on the famous problem of the one and the many: How is it that the world as we know it could be the same, and yet obviously be changing all the time? He knew the answers that Plato and Aristotle had given to that question, but he wanted to examine the original texts themselves. On an unusually warm day in mid-October, he was walking home in the teeming streets of the City. He was perspiring profusely, but he didn't notice the heat because he was trying to phrase an accurate Latin translation for a Greek text he had just read from Heraclitus . . . about the mysterious Logos* that some-

* A Greek term meaning "word," used in many philosophies of that time to represent the meaning of the universe.

how penetrates all things and accounts for the change in things . . . when he became aware of shouts all around him. *Cave!!! Cave!!!* (Watch out! Watch out!).* Surrounded by people running in all directions, when he looked up it was too late for him to move; a chariot, driven by some drunken Praetorian guard, was racing down the street, pulled by two strong Macedonian steeds and heading right for him. He just stood there, paralyzed by the chaos of the moment. He was about to be trampled over when, suddenly, he felt his whole body pushed aside by a powerful force, hurling him to the ground and knocking the wind out of him, as the chariot raced by. He was dazed for a moment, but when he opened his eyes he saw a face looking down on him, that of a young man, about his own age, with a strong build. He had dark eyes and dark complexion, looking like someone from the province of Syria.

Marcus stammered, "I . . . I don't know what to say, but thank you."

The young man looked relieved as Marcus regained his consciousness. "It's all right," he answered with a Palestinian accent, "I'm sorry I had to tackle you." And after saying that, he helped him to his feet.

"May I ask your name?" Marcus asked.

"Dédicus, though my original name was Yeshím."

"And where are you from?"

"From Samaria, in Palestine"

Marcus took him by the hand. "May I repay you in some way . . . ? My father is Gaius Metellus, recently elected Consul of Rome. Maybe you've heard of him."

The young man, who was slightly taller than Marcus, lifted his eyebrows in amazement, and his dark eyes flashed. "Of course. His daughter was just killed a few months ago for being a Christian."

* Since the time of Emperor Augustus, horse-drawn vehicles were prohibited from the streets of Rome during daytime, to allow free transit for pedestrians. Hence the consternation of the people.

Marcus nodded. "But tell me," he said, "what can I give to you? I am most indebted for what you've done."

The young man thought a bit and looked at him closely: "I don't care to receive anything. But answer me this—are you a Christian, as your sister was?"

"Of course not," said Marcus almost indignantly. "I looked into it once and found it to be something irrational, a mere superstition, not connected with any sound philosophy."

At that, Dédicus flinched and looked down at the ground. He said a quick good-bye to Marcus, but added as he left: "Maybe your sister was not so mistaken as you think."

"Wait a minute . . . ," Marcus managed to stammer. "What do you mean? Who are you? . . ." But the young Palestinian had already disappeared into the teeming crowds of Rome.

II.

Justus and his family had not been able to get to the front of the crowds lining the street as Junia was being led to the Colosseum. Several big men right in front of him kept shouting "Whore!" and "Disgrace to your father!" and he could not get in front of them. He felt like challenging them, maybe even hitting them, but then he remembered that the Master whom Junia had spoken of was like a lamb at his execution, and that he had "turned the other cheek." He had prayed that Junia was doing the same at that moment. His wife and children were right beside him, beseeching the Christ for her.

They did not go to the Colosseum, since those of the Way* normally avoided public spectacles unless they went to remove the body of a martyr. Justus had heard that Junia's father had given permission to a group of Christian women to remove his daughter's body and to bury it in a Christian

* A term meaning the Way of Jesus Christ, or Christianity. See Acts of the Apostles 24: 22.

cemetery. Many Christians had praised the nobility of Gaius for that, always considering how sacred the right of burial was in a Roman family.

Though admission to the amphitheater was free that day, as part of Caesar's dole,* Justus and his family decided to return to a small tenement apartment belonging to a friend of theirs near the old Forum, and to pray to Mary the Mother of Jesus, for Junia to keep her faith and courage to the end. Then, as he could see that his children, Timotheus and Carmina, were very sad, he decided to take the whole family for a ride in his fish cart to the countryside along the Via Flaminia. There was a public garden with walking paths there, which many plebeian families made use of on Roman Holidays or when there was a big event in the arena and many businesses were closed.

Justus let his family walk around the garden, while he sat down on a bench. He saw a crow fly from one of the trees nearby, emitting a loud cawing. It reminded him of the birds in his native Pandamum, in northern Latium.** His father had been a farmer, like so many in that area of the Empire; he had not liked Justus's moving to Rome when he was seventeen. "Nothing but thieves," his father had warned him, "and people who have not done an honest day's work in their lives." Justus admired that virtue of the Old Republic,† typified in his father's words; it had made Rome great, when men were responsible and kept their word. It was not so today.

But, like so many other young men, he had wanted to go to the City to make his fortune, to get away from the farm. He had tried doing odd jobs around Rome at first, for he

---

* A monthly rationing of grain for Rome's poorer classes. In a broader sense, the term refers to the general patronage that Roman Emperors gave to the populace of the City, including races and games.

** That part of Italy in which Rome is located.

† The Old Republic refers to the Rome before the Caesars came to power, from the 6th to the 2nd century b.c.; it was a time when individual virtues, family values, and public responsibility were emphasized.

was strong and athletic, but he could get no permanent work. He did not want simply to join the City's mob that survived on Caesar's dole (remembering his father's warning), but, with time on his hands, he began to visit some of the taverns in the Subura section. A few times he had gotten drunk and spent his money, the little that he had, on some of the women there. He felt ashamed of himself, but also helpless to do anything to escape from the situation.

It was then that he had met Constantia. She was the daughter of a fish salesman named Titus Gratius, who lived near the road to Ostia on the Tyrrhenian Sea. One of his friends, a decent chap, had introduced them one day, for he saw that Justus was depressed. *Whatever became of him*, Justus asked himself. *Could he have been a Christian and not said anything, or was he perhaps an angel?* He had liked Constantia from the first. She was of middle height, with reddish brown hair and light brown eyes, though her face was a little pale. She spoke little, but what she said was always thoughtful . . . as if she were thinking about him first, and not herself. He had not seen that in any of the Roman women he had met before.

He was able to begin working for her father, Titus Gratius, at the first steady job he had had, driving the fish cart to Ostia, and bringing freshly caught fish back for markets in Rome. The pay was good; Justus found Titus to be fair in his expectations, even giving him one day off every week. He continued to see Constantia, who helped in the shop with the accounts . . . she was very good at numbers, especially in use of the abacus . . . he had not seen anyone else as deft at it. After much thinking, he decided one day that she would be a good wife for him.

But he had a reservation. Unlike other Roman women he had met, Constantia had not let him become intimate with her. He had at times briefly embraced and kissed her, but when he wanted to become more intimate . . . she would turn away. She never gave any reason for her reaction; she only smiled and said, "We're not married." It made him uncomfortable.

One day, not able to bear the suspense any longer, he asked her if she loved him. Looking at him simply, she said that she did.

"Why don't you give yourself to me, then," he protested. "Why can't I feel your body?"

Constantia looked away from him for a minute. "Justus, have you ever heard of a man named Jesus Christ?" she said softly.

"Of course," Justus answered hotly, wondering what this had to do with anything. "It's a huge superstition. His followers don't honor the Emperor, and somebody told me that they eat someone's body and drink his blood. I knew a few of them once, and they seemed odd to me."

"Justus," Constantia answered him directly, "my father and I are Christians."

He didn't know what to say, and began to shake his head in disbelief. The next day he asked Titus for a leave of absence. He had to think. He had to know what to do. He really did care for Constantia, and her father. They were the best people he had ever met, even better than his own father, who was truthful but rather crusty. How could they have made such a decision to join such a strange group? He knew, also, that they could be denounced and possibly executed. He for one would never denounce them, and he was grateful for Constantia's confidence in him.

He went away for a week, back to Rome; but he had nothing to do. The taverns, the women, were there again, and so was Caesar's dole if he wanted it. But he found, to his wonder, that he didn't want those things. He wanted to go back and see Constantia again, and work for her father. Something deep was working within him. He knew theirs was the better way.

Shortly afterward he returned to Constantia, and began to receive instruction in Christianity from both her and

Titus, and from a Christian priest they knew, who came from Rome; within a year he was baptized and received Communion from the same priest.

As he was remembering those days, his wife and the children were returning from their walk in the park.

"Father," little Carmina said as she rested her head on his shoulder, "what are you thinking about?"

"About how good God is," Justus said simply and gave her a kiss.

III.

Senator Gaius Martellus had always approved of Cynthia's intelligence and common sense. She had been an excellent purchase for his daughter. In the last month of Junia's life, he had hoped that Cynthia might be able to sway her mistress from her attachment to Christianity, but to his chagrin, he had begun to see signs of Christian sympathy in Cynthia herself.

This change made him anxious, and, in the days following Junia's death, he resolved to remove Cynthia from his household as soon as possible. Out of respect for the memory of his daughter, he did not simply want her sold in the slave market to the highest bidder. He resolved to give her to a friend of his, Publius, a rising star in the Senate and rumored to be the Emperor's choice for Consul the following year. What was more, Publius had a daughter, Claudia, who, he thought, would be a good match for Marcus. She was bright and articulate, and known to be quite anti-Christian. The previous year she had been one of the few young people to offer sacrifices at the Temple of Jove on the Capitoline Hill.*

From the beginning, Cynthia did not feel comfortable with her new mistress. Claudia did not have the interest in books and ideas that Junia or Marcia had had; she even made

---

* The shrine in honor of Jupiter, king of the gods, where some of the more ancient ceremonies in the religion of the Romans were conducted.

fun of the Greek philosophers and poets, saying that they all lived in the clouds and had no practical ideas at all. She enjoyed going to the Circus Maximus, the amphitheater games, and to plays with her friends, including Livia; she would often take Cynthia along with her, causing her servant much discomfort. Once she took her to a gladiatorial game, where they sat in one of the upper rows reserved for women. Cynthia did not like having to witness two men fighting to the death with each other. At the end of the match, when one of the gladiators was holding a sword to the throat of the one lying on the ground, Cynthia held her thumb up*— though nobody was paying any attention to her.

Cynthia tried to visit her ailing father as much as possible in the first month she was with Claudia, for his health was failing quickly. Junia had managed to get a better room for him and some good medical attention, but there was nothing the doctors could do for him. Cynthia wanted to spend a few days taking care of him before he died. But she knew that Claudia was a hard mistress, who might not give her permission to leave. She decided to place her request before her anyway. Going timidly to her mistress's chamber, near the end of the courtyard, she bowed to her and said respectfully, "Miss Claudia, I would like to be excused from work for a couple of days."

Claudia looked up quickly from her desk, where she was writing some instructions on a wax tablet. "Why, may I ask?"

"My father is very sick; he may die at any time. I want to be with him."

"Well, *let* the old man die," Claudia retorted. "He's already had far more attention than a slave deserves from the household of Gaius, thanks to you and Junia. It's still the talk of Rome, and it's really absurd."

"But please, Miss Claudia, he's my father. I just want to be with him and to . . ."

---

* The sign of mercy given by the spectators; that is, to spare the life of the fallen gladiator.

"He's a slave," the daughter of Publius interrupted her, "and should get no special treatment. That includes you. Now return to your work."

Cynthia was deeply angered, but she saw that she would be given no favor.

Two days later, her father died. Gaius Metellus, who had a true sense of duty to his late daughter, made sure that the old servant received a decent burial, for a slave; and Claudia had to relent and let Cynthia attend his funeral ceremony. Even Claudia could not deny this right to her, for the duty to pray over one's deceased parents was considered sacred among the Romans; and even slaves were allowed to show such respect for their parents.

Cynthia's father was interred near the Vaticanus Hill, across the Tiber, in a necropolis where some Christians had been buried. Cynthia was moved when she heard the funeral hymns being sung in her native Greek, particularly the hymns to Charon and Pluto, gods of the underworld, even though she did not believe in them anymore.

As she was leaving the gravesite to return to the house of Publius, feeling very depressed and lonely, she noticed a small group of men and women gathered around a red marble monument not far from where her father had been buried. She was particularly surprised because the group included both noble men and women, freedmen, and slaves. It was un-usual to see Patricians* mingle with slaves in a public place.

She decided to wait until all had left, and then she walked over to examine the monument. On it was but one word, painted in Greek characters: PETROS (rock).

"Rock?" the Greek girl asked herself. Why would anyone be called "Rock"? The name seemed absurd to her. She was about to turn away when she became aware of a woman standing a few paces from her. She was around sixty years of age, with fine features, but with sad eyes and a little stoop in her back. It was Scintilla.

* The upper class of Rome; the lower class was called Plebeians.

18

Cynthia lowered her eyes when she saw Scintilla and turned away as if to leave, but the older woman called to her: "Cynthia, don't you remember me?"

Cynthia, though usually calm, felt herself trembling. It was too much for her. First Claudia's cruelty, then her father's death, and now someone who brought back memories of Junia, whom she had truly begun to love in the months before she died . . .

Scintilla saw the tears forming in Cynthia's eyes and ran up and embraced her as if she were her daughter.

After a moment, Cynthia freed herself so she could wipe the tears from her eyes. She didn't want Junia's teacher to see such weakness—but now she had to ask a question that had been on her mind for many weeks.

"Scintilla," Cynthia asked, "did you see her when she was killed?"

"No," Scintilla answered simply, "but I was praying the whole time with a Christian family that Junia knew, so that she would be faithful to the end."

"I am sure she was. You might not know this, Scintilla, but Miss Junia was giving me lessons in Christianity before she was condemned. She was just beginning, and talked often about Jesus' love for all of us, slaves and free. But she didn't mention anything about this Petros. You were just praying here now, weren't you?"

"Oh, Cynthia," Scintilla laughed, "this Petros and his mission come *after* at least twenty-five lessons. But he is part of what Jesus taught."

Cynthia looked at her seriously. She wanted to leave at that moment and not involve herself any further, but something in her soul was making her stay. She thought of Marcia's carefree smile, which had always given her a special joy, and Junia's great kindness to her, and now Scintilla's laughter. There was something wonderful here; she could not go away.

"Scintilla," she said in a very low but serious tone of voice,

"I would like to hear more about the Way. Would you teach me, as you did Miss Junia?"

IV.

For several days after he was shoved out of the path of the careening chariot, Marcus kept thinking about the event. He still lived in a mental daze, but had the kind of mind that cannot rest until it knows the truth behind things. What most amazed him was that there could be a man who had risked his own life to save him, and had not wanted any compensation or reward for what he had done. That seemed really absurd to Marcus, for it was well known that, in Rome, every man—and woman—could be bought for a price.

Marcus felt that his mind was being plagued by those parting words of the Samaritan. He had said, "Maybe your sister was right," or something like that. Right about what? he asked himself. About Christianity? About somebody who could rise from the dead? About an all-powerful God that would allow himself to be crucified? About eating and drinking someone's body and blood to obtain eternal life?

They were all ideas that he had heard before; some of them were related to mystery religions like the Mithra* from the East . . . but he had rejected them all. He could see mockeries of the Christians every day on the street. He had even been broad minded enough to attend classes with the Christian philosopher Justin, in order to investigate Christianity, despite his sister's objections. But he was not satisfied with what he heard. It was too much for any rational man to accept.

And then there was the other idea that Junia had once given him: that her god was really a lover. Certainly, he had

* A mystery religion from the eastern part of the Empire, which involved the worship of a sun-god and his slaying of an animal that brought salvation to mankind.

reasoned, that could not be the god of Plato or Aristotle, or the Stoic god. A lover? Who cares for every human being, rich or poor? It would be impossible! But then it had occurred to him—that *some* god must have cared for him that day when he was about to be killed by a chariot, and when a fellow his own age had risked his own life to save him. Was that perhaps a sign of some god's loving him?

As Marcus sat under the poplar tree in the courtyard of his home one morning, reflecting on these things, Numo, one of his father's personal slaves, came up to him. "Excuse me, Master Marcus," he said politely. "Your father wishes to speak to you in his study."

Marcus rose dutifully and went to his father's chamber, where he kept his scrolls and correspondence. Gaius had just dismissed his *clientes*, and Marcus could hear them leaving the big stone house with its marble trimmings, conversing excitedly with one another, and each going to carry out the assignment that Gaius had given him. One of their number, Bombolinus, almost bumped into Marcus.

"Don't you ever slow down, Bombo?" Marcus said—but he received only a slight bow as answer.

Gaius was seated at his marble working table, preparing a speech for the Senate. Now, as Consul, he no longer had to prosecute or defend legal cases, but he had a much more important task to do: to present the Emperor's will to the members of the Senate, and to get them to agree to it. In this, he had to take into account the ideas and feelings of each of them. He knew them all well. The message had to be clear, but flexible enough to allow each senator to feel satisfied and to vote yes.

Marcus paused for a moment in the doorway before entering his father's study, and looked at him. Though it had been only a few months since Junia's death, he had aged considerably. He had always been a serious-looking man, but now his face looked sad, as if there were a great weight on his soul. Yet he never revealed his inner feelings to anybody, not to his son, not even to his wife. It was part of his Stoic cast of mind.

"You sent for me, Father?" Marcus said briefly.

"Yes, Marcus. I will get to the point quickly. You are now in your twenty-first year, and have expressed no desire to be married. You must consider perpetuating the family name."

Lost in his world of theses and classes, Marcus had not been thinking of marriage. He had had intimacy with a few women already in his life—a common practice among Patrician young men at the time. One of those liaisons, with a Sybellian priestess, had caused considerable scandal for his family a few years before, It had particularly hurt his sister and his father. But he had no desire to marry. A wife would only be a burden, and he could get his occasional pleasure here and there, without having to pay such a price.

"I hadn't thought much about it, Father"

"Please do," his father answered him quickly. "Time is going by, and the name Metellus Cimber must continue. I would like you to meet a certain young woman who I think would be a good match for you."

Marcus hesitated. He did not want to face such a complication at this time, but he respected his father's wishes. Many of his colleagues had already asked him the same. So he answered simply, "Yes, Father, and who is this woman?"

"Claudia, daughter of Senator Publius, who will probably be appointed Consul next year. She is a very intelligent and practical young woman . . . and therefore will be a big help to you, so wrapped up in your books. She knows how to run a household very efficiently, and has the proper attitude toward slaves and Christians. She is fairly attractive too."

Marcus had met Claudia, and he knew her to be one of Livia's friends, who had conspired with her mother to expose Junia as a Christian.

"Are you aware, Father, that she is one of Livia's friends?"

"Only a friend, Marcus," Consul Gaius answered. "As far

as I know, or any one else, she did not participate in having Junia condemned."

"But she probably approved of it, since she's known to be quite vocal against the Christians."

"And what is wrong with that?" Gaius responded irritably. For a moment he lost his practiced Stoic attitude. "She'll keep you from falling into your sister's tragic mistake."

Marcus saw that his father's logic was clear and sensible, and he could not dispute it. He was frightened by Christianity, and by what it could do to people; he had no desire to get near it.

So he agreed to see Claudia.

V.

Claudia, daughter of Senator Publius, was a fairly tall woman with light brown hair and clear hazel-colored eyes. She was something of a leader among marriageable young women in Rome because of her sharp wit and practical skill in getting things done. She was also very ambitious, wanting to rise as far as she could in Rome's social classes. So she was delighted to hear of the interest that Gaius had in matching her with his son, Marcus. She had often joked at parties about Marcus's "theoretical ways," but she now resolved to change her approach to him. She hired a private tutor from the Athenaeum, where Marcus studied, to instruct her in the ideas of Plato, Aristotle, the Epicureans, and the Stoics. She even forced herself to learn a few Greek words and phrases in order to impress Marcus.

On the afternoon of their first meeting, Marcus arrived, as he always did, walking in the middle of the street among the Plebeians—but he had put on his best toga, its purple border showing his rank as a Patrician. Claudia wore her most costly silk stola, adorned with a broach of brown opals that matched the color of her hair.

After walking half way up the Quirinal Hill, where

Publius had his mansion, and entering into the front courtyard, Marcus was surprised to see Cynthia standing slightly behind Claudia. His father had not told him what settlement he had arranged for the slave girl. He smiled approvingly at Cynthia, because she had served his sister and his family so well, and was so level-headed. She wore the simple white tunic appropriate to slaves, though he did note the pretty white chrysanthemum in her dark hair.

Claudia noticed that Marcus was perspiring a bit from his walk, something inappropriate to be seen in a Patrician, but she said nothing. She smiled at him graciously, and led him to the inner courtyard, where there was a marble fountain her father had recently imported from Dalmatia. It had at its center a gold-covered faun whose mouth was spewing out water. Nearby were busts of Claudia's parents, with perforations in the pupils of their eyes, as was the custom of sculptors under Hadrian, in order to increase realism.

Claudia bade her servant girl to bring them some figs and two goblets of wine.

Before speaking to Marcus, she looked carefully at him. He was of middle height, a little stocky in build, with dreamy blue eyes. His hair, like hers, was light brown, and his face had a resolute jaw like his father's.

"Oh, Marcus," she said casually, as if she did it every day, "I was reading a bit of Aristotle yesterday. I'm not sure that I can agree with the solution he proposes to the problem of the one and the many."

Marcus's interest was awakened, and his eyes showed his interest. "Do you mean his theory of act and potency?"

"Exactly," chimed in Claudia, and after she had spoken just a little about it (she had just heard of it the night before), Marcus proceeded to explain it in full detail, with Aristotle's original words, clarifying how it was not a bad effort to solve a philosophical conundrum left to the world by philosophers before Socrates.

Claudia listened to him with apparent interest, every once

in a while asking a question so that Marcus might think she was quite informed on the issue. When Cynthia entered with the figs and the wine, Marcus stopped speaking for a moment and smiled at her. Claudia was somewhat jealous of that smile. She knew, of course, that Cynthia had been Junia's servant, but didn't know that Marcus had a liking for her.

The dinner brought in by Publius's servants was elaborate, accompanied by music performed by Egyptian flautists. Publius, a rather lean man with crafty eyes, joined them. He exchanged pleasantries with Marcus about the fall weather and tried to get some of Marcus's views on the political situation at the time . . . but he found that Marcus's answers were very vague, and that he didn't even know the names of the more important senators. *He's a dreamer*, Publius thought to himself; but he would be an excellent match for his daughter, both politically and financially. Besides, Claudia probably could twist him around her little finger.

Later in the evening, after the sun had set, Claudia dismissed Cynthia and the other servants, and invited Marcus to take a stroll with her in the spacious courtyard. There was a cool evening breeze, and the overhead stars were bright. They both had drunk a great deal of wine. Claudia felt that she had made a good impression on Marcus . . . both she and her father . . . but she wanted to win him over completely. After blowing softly in his ear and whispering an invitation to him, she gently took his arm and began to lead him to her chamber.

She could feel Marcus stiffen, and he stopped. He had had affairs with women before, but after Junia's death he had not gone with any woman, out of respect for his deceased sister. He had always admired her clean life, unlike that of many other young women of her rank; and he was proud that she had died a virgin. He would not go with Claudia to her room, though he felt quite attracted to her at that moment.

"No," he said quickly, "it's getting late. I have a new manuscript to read before tomorrow's class. Thank you for your hospitality. We shall see each other again."

VI.

The day after his visit with Claudia, Marcus was walking toward the Athenaeum on the Capitoline Hill. He was dressed now in a simple tunic, but was wrapped also in a red cape because of the chill. He carried two scrolls under his right arm. He had borrowed them from the large library that Caesar Augustus had built a hundred and fifty years earlier. They were writings of Philo, a Jew from Alexandria who had written about the relationship of ancient Jewish writings and those of the Greek philosophers of his time. Marcus's Jewish colleague Syphon had recommended that he read them, and he was finding them fascinating.

As he ascended the steps of the large building, with its light-green columns, he saw, at the top of the stairs, a familiar face, a face he would never forget. It was that of the young Palestinian Dédicus. Marcus felt a surge of gratitude and affection swelling in his heart, and went quickly up the steps to greet him.

"Dédicus, Dédicus," he called. "Do you remember me?"

The dark-skinned youth smiled immediately and came down the stairway to greet Marcus, though there were many other students thronging past them. They greeted each other in the Roman style, with a firm mutual grip on the right forearms.

"I owe you *something*," said Marcus, smiling warmly, "and I would like to get to know you better. You ran off too quickly the other day. May I invite you to some wine at the tavern on the Via Nomentina?"

"I was about to hear Sapion's lecture."

"Sapion?" Marcus said derisively. "He repeats himself all the time. Just skip it for today; I assure you, you'll hear the same tomorrow."

Dédicus laughed in agreement, and the two young men went down the steps to a nearby street. It was the beginning of the day, so they had no trouble finding a couple of benches and a free table.

"Tell my about yourself, Dédicus. You said that you were from Samaria. As I recall, that is between the regions of Judaea and Galilee in Palestine. A very troubled part of the world these days."

"Yes, that "trouble" is one of the reasons I left and came to Rome. A Judaean by name of Bar Kochba has been stirring up a group of Jewish zealots there against the Roman occupation, especially in Jerusalem.* A lot of men from my land have joined him, even though many Jews consider us a bastard race. If I had stayed, I would have been forced to join them."

"I take it you're not a fighter," observed Marcus.

"If it were a cause I agreed with and understood, I would fight. But for now I prefer to study and to find out if there is any truth worth fighting for."

Marcus looked at him with surprise. He had never heard of truth spoken about in that way. A truth to discuss, to speculate about, to apply to one's life, possibly . . . but a truth to fight for, or die for? That seemed too much to him.

"I have never met such a truth," he said honestly. "There are times when I think that there is no truth, based on all of the conflicting theories I've heard."

Dédicus smiled self-consciously, looking down at his mug of wine. He said in a low voice, "Well, I have found something that looks promising."

Marcus eyed him inquisitively. "One of the newer Stoic or Platonist systems, perhaps?"

"Did you ever hear of a philosopher named Justin? For a

* In A.D. 135, Hadrian's troops turned Jerusalem into a secular city called Aelia, and built a large temple to the god Jupiter in the middle of the city; the Jews who still lived there considered this act a blasphemy.

brief time he was giving some lessons here before returning to the East. He's actually from my homeland." *

"Yes," Marcus said. And he remembered how he had upset his sister when he had told her for the first time that he was considering this Justin's ideas. "Yes, I attended some lectures by him, but he didn't convince me. He's a Christian, you know."

"Well," Dédicus replied, "I'm looking at some of his writings very carefully. I have not met him personally, but I am reading two or three texts that he has finished recently. They show that the message of Christianity is a fulfillment of some of Aristotle's and Plato's great insights."

"That's impossible," Marcus objected. "How could Christianity be related to Aristotle's and Plato's ideas? It is based on the irrational premise that God could become a man and, even more irrationally, that he could die on a cross." And again he remembered some of his heated conversations with Junia about that very topic.

But Dédicus was not impressed. "If the Christian God is truly all-powerful and the Creator of the world as we know it, why could he not become a man without ceasing to be God? Why could he not die on a cross in order to save us, if he chose to?"

Marcus could not give him an answer to that, but as they parted they agreed to continue the discussion; there, at the same tavern, at the same time, one week later.

VII.

Marcus kept meeting with Dédicus, once, sometimes twice, a week; their friendship was growing fast. Sometimes they would meet at one of the taverns; other times they would

* Historical sources say that St. Justin made two journeys to Rome. The period of his second journey and residence there was the longer, from A.D. 138 to 165, when he established a school; he was martyred during the time of Emperor Marcus Aurelius.

walk around one of the public parks near the Athenaeum. When spring began, Marcus invited him to spend a few days at his family's villa in northeastern Latium—where Junia had discovered the news of Marcia's death the year before. They went horseback riding together; it was one of Marcus's few athletic interests, and he was good at it. Dédicus was not accustomed to horses, though he had ridden camels and donkeys in Samaria and Judaea. Giving him an easier horse at first, Marcus showed him how to sit properly and keep his balance while riding.

But if Dédicus learned about horsemanship from Marcus, Marcus was receiving insights in philosophy from Dédicus—he was amazed at the Palestinian's grasp of Plato and Aristotle, particularly by his contention that the human mind could grasp a permanent truth, and even guide one's life by it. Dédicus would frequently weave the Hebrew Scriptures in with philosophical ideas about man and happiness. And he was also pointing to a God who was much more personal than the Olympian gods, or the concepts of Aristotle, Plato, or the Stoics. To Marcus's discomfort, Dédicus also spoke of a demanding God, who established a moral law and would judge men by it. But as he thought about it more, Marcus could understand how it was perfectly reasonable that the same God who made everything could also determine the standard for achieving true happiness.

"Dédicus," Marcus asked one day, while walking outside of the Athenaeum when they had returned to classes, "you're a mystery to me."

"Do you mean in some of my philosophical ideas?"

"No," Marcus answered, "those are clear enough, and I'm beginning to agree with you on some of them. But it's your personal life. I've noticed that when we go to the tavern, you never have more than two flasks of wine . . . and you never talk about women. I find that strange. You're still young . . ."

29

The thought had occurred to Marcus that Dédicus might be one of the large homosexual population that lived in Rome, but he preferred not to bring up the topic directly.

Dédicus, whose dark eyes were usually quite intense, relaxed a bit and began to laugh. "Oh, never fear, Marcus. I like wine well enough, and find women quite attractive . . . Be assured of that. But I have been discovering something more compelling in life."

"More compelling than . . . women? It would have to be a very powerful truth, then."

"It is," answered Dédicus simply. "As a matter of fact, it is more than a truth. It's a person."

"A person who has more attraction to you than wine or women? And it's not a man either?"

"It *is* a man."

"Oh ho!" Marcus said maliciously. "So you are of that persuasion after all!"

Dédicus colored at that, and Marcus saw his friend's face flash with anger. "Marcus, one can love a man for who he is, not only in a sexual way. There are many kinds of love, as Aristotle himself states. Not all love is eros." *

Recognizing the truth of his friend's response, Marcus regretted his hasty remark. "Well, Dédicus, I would like to meet this personal friend of yours, since he seems to mean so much to you."

Dédicus stopped short, as if struck by a sudden thought. "Yes, I hope you will meet him someday. He's the one who inspired me to save you from the racing chariot."

---

* *Eros* according to Aristotle and other Greek philosophers was the lowest kind of love between human beings, lowest because it was based on sensual attraction and pleasure.

VIII.

Justus often had to work at night, for fish and produce traffic were prohibited during the daytime in the streets of Rome. His schedule was to pick up a load of fish in the port of Ostia,* and then drive the fifteen miles or so to Rome and deliver them to customers. This business, which he had learned from Constantia's father and had inherited after his death, was a source of good income: there were many fish vendors in Rome, and they did not have the time or equipment to obtain fish to sell each day. Justus had two large carts for transporting fish and sometimes grain, drawn by two strong horses that he kept in a field just behind his home outside Rome.

He kept careful count of the types of fish he hauled, for each type had a different market price; usually sea fish brought a much higher price than river fish. He always tried to be fair in the prices he charged the fish vendors (it would have been easy to cheat—many times he was their only provider); most of them were located at the Fish Forum (*Forum piscarium*) or on the Via Biberatica, which was also called Trajan's Market, in the heart of commercial Rome. Sometimes, as a personal loss, he would reduce the price or give free supplies of fish to vendors who had large families or who were particularly impoverished.

As a Christian, he took a great satisfaction in his work, though it was looked down on by the noble classes of the City, the Patricians and the Equestrians. He knew that Christ had chosen mostly fishermen to spread his kingdom a hundred years before. As a distributor, Justus had to deal with fishermen constantly... of all sorts and from all ports ... most of them big rough men with foul mouths. He would have to haggle and argue with them in order to pay

* Ostia, a seaport located at the mouth of the Tiber on the Tyrrhenian Sea, was noted for receiving shipments of food from around the world. It was connected to Rome by the Via Portuensis.

them a reasonable price; and once, he had gotten into a fist fight with a brawny supplier from Gaul—which he had won.

It gave him a certain satisfaction to know that he was providing a direct service for thousands of people in Rome each day; and as he drove into the City, he would pray for the people who were sleeping, or at least trying to sleep, in their crowded tenement apartments. He prayed that someday they might all get to know Christ and his teachings, the joy of his and his family's life.

Among his customers was Discalus, whose fish shop was near the beginning of the Via Biberatica, not far from the old Forum. He felt sorry for him. His wife had died about two years before, and he seemed to be lonely and embittered about life. He had not sought to remarry. Often, when Justus brought his supply of fish, he would tell Discalus a joke or funny story that he had heard from the fishermen about their travels, or a remembrance from his native town of Turnia, as Discalus also was from that part of Italy. Discalus's young son, Gaius, was very bright and had a forthright and courageous spirit to him, which Justus liked to see.

As they became closer friends, Justus decided to invite Discalus to his home one evening. He thought that this might cheer him up a bit. What's more, he wanted his son, Timotheus, to meet Gaius, though Timotheus was three years older. As he was driving Discalus and his son to his house on the road to Ostia for the main meal of the day—in the early afternoon—Discalus began to talk about the Christians.

"I just cannot understand them," he said. "They seem so stubborn in their ways. Look for instance at that young woman Junia, who was beheaded a few months ago. Rich, smart, beautiful, with all kinds of admirers . . . and she throws it all away for some mythical person who died on a cross. What a suffering she caused to her father, Gaius the Consul."

Gaius began to squirm in his seat when his father spoke that way about Junia. He had seen her in the chariot and had admired her bravery, if only for an instant, as she was being led to the amphitheater. But he said nothing, so as not to contradict his father.

Justus himself didn't know what to say. He would have loved for Discalus to understand more about the Way, but this was not the time. And so he said, "If you get to know some of them, I think you wouldn't consider them so stubborn. And their founder was not a myth, but a real person who was crucified in Judaea under Pontius Pilate about a hundred years ago."

"Yes, I know," Discalus answered. "But do you know what they believe? They say that this Jesus rose from the dead, and that he's going to raise all of his followers one day. They also say that their priests are able to convert bread and wine into his body and blood. Have you ever heard of anything so incredible?"

"Well," Justus said weakly, "I guess that is hard to believe" but in his heart he was praying that someday Discalus would believe it.

Constantia had prepared a pleasant dinner in the kitchen next to the small triclinum that served as the dining room. The room was not so elaborate as the ones of wealthy families, but there was a colorful fresco on the wall, a country scene, showing a brown stallion galloping over a hilltop, with a blue sky in the background. Discalus liked it immediately. It reminded him of the countryside where he grew up.

Justus had no servants, so Timotheus and Carmina served the dishes and cleared the platters when they were done. The chicken, the figs, and the pudding were excellent, and Discalus remarked to himself how good a cook Constantia was, as his deceased wife had been also: she could make ordinary porridge, made of water and wheat grains, into a real delight.

After the meal, as they were still savoring the vintage wine that Justus had purchased for the occasion, Carmina brought out a lyre, which Justus had given her for her last birthday. With a young girl's ingenuity and some help from her mother, she had learned the instrument quickly, and she sang an old Roman country song that her father had taught her when she was very little. Music seemed to come naturally to her, and her dark brown eyes shone brightly as she sang. Since her father had told her that he was praying that Discalus and his son might someday become Christians, she said a silent prayer for both of them after she finished singing.

IX.

Half way up the Aventine Hill was an estate built by a cloth merchant in the time of the Emperor Nerva.* This merchant had led a rather solitary life and had never married; when he died, he left no heirs, so his home was put up for public sale by the City authorities. As Marcus and Dédicus walked toward it, Marcus noticed that it was not extravagant, but was well cared for. There was a fairly large courtyard in front, with a rectangular pool bordered by poplar trees.

"Who is the owner now?" Marcus asked his friend.

"Numer and his friends purchased it about a year ago."

"Who is Numer?"

"You'll soon meet him," answered Dédicus; he raised his eyebrows with a glimmer in his eye . . . something unlike his usual serious expression. He had been speaking to Marcus about Numer and his friends for several weeks, and was at last bringing him to see them.

As they entered the atrium, it was around the tenth hour of the day.** The fellows who owned the house had just left

---

* Nerva ruled beween A.D. 96 and 98.

** Since the Romans measured the hours of the day from sunrise (around six A.M.), the tenth hour was about four o'clock in the afternoon. Supper (*cena*) was eaten at either three or four o'clock in the afternoon, and often a period of singing or other entertainment followed.

the rather small dining room and were sitting in the atrium on small floor-cushions or wooden stools. Marcus surmised that they did not have the funds to buy other furnishings. There were eight of them. In the middle of the group was a rather short, stout African man playing a flute. One of them was singing; he looked like a native of Greece or Macedonia: he was fairly tall, and had a short, well-trimmed black beard. Despite his good appearance, his singing was off key in many verses, but the African was so good at the flute that he seemed to make up for the singer's faults. Once in a while, if the singer hit a discordant note, the flautist himself made a discordant note—to the great merriment of the others.

Marcus immediately had a good feeling about this group, as he and Dédicus sat down. They were all young men, about his age, though the African seemed a little older. Most seemed to be from Italy or Gaul, but one fellow in perhaps his middle twenties had fair skin with blonde hair; Marcus guessed that he might be from Germania, perhaps a freed slave. He saw a couple of togas folded and lying nearby on the marble floor—so he knew that at least two of them were citizens of Rome like himself.

After the singer and flautist concluded, another stood up and put on his toga. The toga had a purple stripe along its border, so Marcus knew that this one was a member of the noble class. He had a beard that was both curled and oiled, as was the custom among upper-class men in Hadrian's time. Marcus himself had never wanted to follow that fashion with his beard, and his father, being of simple Stoic taste, had agreed with his decision. Marcus thought the fellow was going to give some kind of public discourse, but what he said was instead some kind of parody about people from Gaul. It was based on a text from Caesar's history of the Gallic Wars, but some of the words were changed to make jokes and plays on words. In describing Gallic houses, one particularly funny part of the parody spoke of a Gaul who wanted to build a house along a river, but the house kept collapsing on his head.

"What's all this about?" Marcus whispered to his friend.

"It's a celebration for Atticus, who was born in Gaul and would like to be an architect. Titus is studying oratory, and he's poking fun at him, using Julius Caesar's text as the basis for a joke." And then he pointed to Atticus, a wiry-looking fellow with olive skin and a thoughtful face, sitting in the middle of the group. He didn't seem to be annoyed by Titus's remarks, but laughed good-naturedly with the others when jokes were told about his countrymen.

After the reading, two other fellows, athletic in build, got up and went to the middle of the atrium. They both put on round helmets, and their short tunics came to about the middle of their thighs, like those of the gladiators. But their "swords" they had fashioned from two papyrus scrolls cut to a point. Both of them lifted their swords to the spectators and solemnly said, in a loud voice, "*Papyrituri te salutamus*." * They then engaged in a mock combat, dancing around the atrium and striking their paper swords together. The other fellows were roaring with laughter, as one or the other of the combatants feigned a mortal wound. After a time of this playing, Numer got up from the floor, went behind one of the fighters, and deftly managed to trip him. With that, everyone laughed again, and then all agreed it was time to leave.

Marcus was amazed. He had never seen such a spectacle, and it was all in fun. Unlike the normal city entertainments in the theaters, there had been no obscene stories or scenes, and no blood was shed. In fact, he could see that it was a very deliberate satire of the gladiatorial games, which so many people took so seriously. He had laughed so hard at their antics that he thought his Stoic father would be ashamed of him. And for the whole time, he had forgotten

---

* Literally, "About to be *papyrused*, we salute you," a nonce word forming a humorous parody of the phrase the gladiators used before their mortal combat: *Morituri te salutamus*, "About to die, we salute you."

about those philosophical issues that had been obsessing his thoughts in recent weeks.

As the group left the atrium, they smiled in a friendly way to Dédicus and Marcus, as if to say, "Any friend of Dédicus is a friend of ours." Dédicus took Marcus to meet Numer, the short African fellow who seemed to be the the group's chief comic and ringleader.

"Numer," Dédicus said, "I'd like you to meet Marcus Metellus Cimber. He is the son of Consul Gaius Metellus."

Numer's dark eyes opened wide with surprise at first, but then he laughed, showing a splendid arrangement of ivory-white teeth—and made a deep bow. "I suppose, then," he said with an Egyptian accent, "that we should call you Master Marcus."

"Oh, no," Marcus answered simply, "just Marcus."

X.

The following day, after classes at the Athenaeum, Marcus asked Dédicus more about the group he had just met, as they were walking back to Dédicus's apartment on the Via Biberatica. He lived on the fourth floor in a very small room.

"I cannot remember having such a good time in my whole life, Dédicus. It was amazing; last night, I actually went to sleep laughing. Who are those fellows, anyway?"

"They're all students or apprentices of some sort. Some study philosophy, others law, others architecture. And as you can see, they're the best of friends."

"Do they all live there?"

"Some live there, some with their families."

"How long have you known them?"

"For about a year now. Titus, the one who did the humorous reading from Caesar's history, introduced me. Since I was interested in philosophy and ideas, he told me that I had to meet some of these fellows."

"Well, I didn't see much philosophy or ideas yesterday; that's for sure."

"I'll have to take you another day, and you'll hear lots of ideas, especially from Numer and Titus. They actually are speaking with several students who go to Aventine once a week.

"Aventine? Is that what they call the place?"

"Yes, logically, because it's on the Aventine Hill."

"I would love to go to some of their gatherings"

"Well, let's go Thursday evening after supper. Numer is going to speak about Parmenides' concept of the One and how that connects with the Hebrew sacred writings."

"We have spoken about that a number of times."

"Yes, Marcus, and most of those ideas I got from Numer."

———

On Thursday evening, after a quick supper together in the City, the two friends started to walk toward the Aventine. Dédicus told Marcus about Numer. He had been born in Alexandria, which was one of the centers of Greek learning and ideas in the Eastern Empire, along with Antioch. Marcus had gone to Alexandria four years before, and had visited one of its famous libraries. Numer, Dédicus continued, was about thirty years old, and had never married. He was also a good friend of Justin, who had given lectures in Rome the year before

"Do you mean the Justin who spoke about Christianity?"

"Yes."

"As I told you before, I also met him and studied under him, but I was not convinced by his ideas."

"Maybe Numer will convince you."

"What do you mean? Is Numer a Christian?"

Dédicus hesitated a minute. Marcus could see his lips moving slowly, as if he were praying something silently. He looked at Marcus a little bashfully. "Marcus, all those fellows at the Aventine house are Christians. They meet there regularly to study, to pray, and to enjoy each other's company."

Marcus stopped short in his walk but said nothing for a moment. He stroked his beard, always slightly unkempt. "So that's it! The sense of joy they had . . . and their concern for one another. It entertained me, and frightened me at the same time."

"What do you mean?"

"It's the same joy and care I saw in my sister, and in her friend Marcia. I could never figure it out."

"Maybe there are some things you shouldn't try to figure out."

Dédicus moved as if to keep walking forward to the Aventine, but Marcus stood still. He hesitated to go any farther.

"It's all too much for me, Dédicus," he said. "I have to think. I don't know . . . I don't think I should get involved anymore."

Dédicus looked at him apologetically. "I'm sorry, Marcus. I should have told you sooner. But I wanted you to meet them. I understand your reaction."

"Are you a Christian, too, Dédicus?"

"No, but I hope to become one next year, at the Easter Vigil, which is the big Christian feast day."

XI.

For the first time in his life, Marcus felt totally confused and helpless. He had always been able to conceptualize things well—this way of thinking gave him a sense of control of his life— and he had always thought that he was a pretty good judge of human nature. But this whole series of events that he had experienced—his life being saved so suddenly; his conversations with Dédicus, who seemed to be the first actual friend he had ever had; the tremendous new insights he was receiving about philosophy and the possibility of a permanent Truth; and most recently this fascinating group of Christians at the house on the Aventine—was beyond him. He felt that some great Power had suddenly changed the rules without his knowledge and consent.

One part of him was greatly attracted by what he had seen in Dédicus and Numer; he desired to know more about Christianity, and to share in the courage and daring these people obviously had. He desired to share their joy, as Junia had in the last year of her life—and as he could not explain.

But another part of him told him that this whole path was very dangerous, that he should go his own way and stay far away from Christianity. He did not want to end up like his sister. The weeks went by, and he did nothing. When he saw Dédicus at the Athenaeum, he avoided him, though he felt like a coward in doing so. He kept turning over the whole question in his mind, but with no resolution.

In the meantime, Cynthia, Claudia's servant, began to see Scintilla for instruction in the Christian faith, as Junia had. They met in the servants' quarters behind the kitchen at the house of Scintilla's new master, Appius, who had made a fortune in precious gems. Scintilla found the girl to be a very attentive and intelligent student; her questions were so deep that she decided to ask one of the priests in Rome, Father Anacletus, to instruct Cynthia in some of the lessons. One of her questions was: How could Jesus be both God and man? Another was: How could he be equal to the Father if in some way he had come from the Father? The priest explained to her that a better vocabulary had to be found to explain these mysteries better, that some Christian writers were working on it, but that there were also those who were inventing strange explanations that made the Son inferior to the Father. These were the Gnostics,* and they were confusing things a great deal and deceiving many Christians, especially around Alexandria.

---

* Gnostics: from the Greek word *gnosis*, "knowledge." The Gnostics spoke of a "secret" kind of knowledge that would liberate a person from the evil of matter.

As Cynthia progressed in her knowledge, she also began to practice what she heard. As a slave, she understood humility and service well, but the concepts of charity and forgiveness were still hard for her to grasp. She could not forgive the Roman soldiers who had brought her and her father to Rome when she was only six years old. It was also very hard for her, as she confided to Scintilla one day, to be pleasant and conscientious with her new mistress, Claudia, who was very demanding and unreasonable, and had refused to let her see her father in the days before he died. One time, Claudia had even had her whipped for a small offense. Junia would never have done so. At times Cynthia felt a hatred for Claudia arising in her heart.

"No, you must not give into that," the older woman rebuked her. "Don't forget what Jesus said: we must love our enemies, and do good to those who hate us."

"That's very hard to do at times, Scintilla."

"I hope you will try to understand her better, Cynthia. Put yourself in her situation—though, of course, she is very wealthy and has many privileges. Consider if she has ever had any happiness in her life, if she has ever had a friend. Consider if she has ever sought for anything beyond money, pleasure, or getting ahead in the world. She's blind and helpless in many ways; and maybe, through your prayer and service to her, you can bring her to Christ."

"Scintilla, that's exactly what Junia was doing for me the last six months of her life!"

"Well, Cynthia, you must return the service to Claudia."

XII.

When Cynthia returned home that morning, Claudia was busy having the kitchen slaves prepare a special feast for Marcus. She had not seen much of him in some three months; she was quite annoyed, and also fearful that she might be losing his interest. And the few times that Marcus had come to visit her, he had seemed even more abstracted than usual . . . as if he were struggling with something inside of him. He wasn't paying attention to her. She hoped this to be the night to get a decision from him.

"Why are you so late, Cynthia?" she snapped at her servant as she walked into the atrium.

"Miss Claudia, I told you that I would be out until midday once a week, and you gave me permission."

"Never mind. Help to prepare the flautist with his music, and make sure the singer pronounces the Greek correctly for the after-dinner entertainment . . . he's really from Sicily, not Greece. And then come to my chamber to help me with my hair."

Claudia wanted her hair done in the most fashionable and attractive way, braided and rolled around her head like a crown, with generous bits of gold dust on top. She had hired cosmeticians from Egypt to paint her eyebrows and lips, and had put on her most costly necklace, the one with its smooth white pearls, and earrings to match. She also wore her most beautiful light-blue stola, trimmed with threads of gold.

When Marcus came, he also was dressed very well, and he had even trimmed his beard; but he was perspiring as always, for he refused to be carried in a litter.

During the meal, Claudia spoke about recent news from the streets—her friend Livia was about to be married; and many said that it was the last year for old Julianus the Consul; and many were wondering whom Hadrian was grooming for his successor—some said Antoninus. When these topics sparked no response, she tried to bring up some ideas from the neo-Platonists—but Marcus was pondering another theme. Finally, she simply asked him if he liked her hair and make-up.

At that the son of Gaius looked at her more attentively: "Claudia, I thank you sincerely for your efforts to please me. You are truly lovely to look at, but please consider that real beauty is not so much in the body as in the spirit."

The daughter of Publius was mystified by his words. He said them so gently that she could not take offense, but at the same time she felt that he was rejecting her in some way. She had made the effort to be gracious during the whole meal, but she could no longer contain her annoyance.

"Marcus," she said impatiently, "I cannot go on forever like this. I have my life to lead, and you have to decide soon. Your father is also becoming impatient with your behavior. Will you agree to marry me, or not?"

The brother of Junia looked down at the figs in the silver platter in front of him. He took one, dipped it in the sauce bowl, ate it quickly, and then looked directly into the clear hazel brown eyes of Claudia.

"Claudia, I can't give you an answer right now. I'm searching for something, and I think I'm about to find it. Please be patient with me. It should not take me very long."

Claudia slapped a hand on the table; tears were beginning to form in her eyes. "What are you "searching" for, Marcus? You're the son of Gaius Metellus, Consul of Rome. You have all the opportunities before you. You have my love, which I give to you freely. You will have my dowry, which your father has already arranged with my father. What else can you be searching for? You're being very unfair to me!"

And as Marcus hesitated to say anything, but just looked at her helplessly, she quickly rose from the table, called for Cynthia to escort her, and left the room, infuriated.

Marcus knew he had to decide soon about Claudia. He could not let more weeks go by. He grasped the basic justice of Claudia's outburst. Yes, she was domineering, she had a temper, but she was being honest with him. He was deeply touched at her efforts to learn a little bit of philosophy for his sake. And she was attractive and knew how to get things done—and he concluded that she would be a good wife. But . . . he had to solve the question looming in his mind; it would not go away.

The next day, he met Dédicus at the Athenaeum, apologized for avoiding him for so many weeks, and told him he wanted to talk with Numer about Christianity. He would commit himself to nothing, he warned, but he did want to start learning about it.

XIII.

Marcus arranged his schedule so that he had time to see Numer and Atticus twice a week. He was ready for the opportunity to learn more about Christianity, but also about philosophy, for Numer was from Alexandria, one of the more sophisticated and intellectual cities in the Roman Empire. When Numer began to explain Christ from a philosophical point of view, Marcus was impressed. Atticus, being from Gaul, was more concrete in his explanation of Christianity, and spoke above all about the life of Jesus and his miracles. Marcus noted that his two teachers completed each other well.

"Tell me what Christians understand by the Logos," Marcus asked Numer on his first day, as he had begun by speaking about Jesus Christ as the savior of all men. Marcus had been thinking about this mysterious concept for some years, especially because his father, a Stoic, believed in a Logos or Word that bound all things together through necessity.

"From the writings of the first followers of Christ, whom Jesus called apostles," the Alexandrian answered, "the Word or Logos is the Son of God the Father, sent to the world to bring all men into unity with himself, the Father, and the Holy Spirit. He is all-knowing and all-mighty, just as the Father and the Holy Spirit are."

"But if he is the *Son* of the Father, is he not in some way inferior? That is, is he not younger or did he not come after the Father?"

"No, we believe that the Son also is eternal, and divine, just as the Father is. As a matter of fact, one of the apostles, John, who lived not far from Ephesus for the last years of his life, has stated in one of his writings that 'In the beginning the Word, and the Word was with God, and the Word was God,' and 'all things were made through him.'" *

"It sounds quite like the Logos or Constituting Fire of the Stoics, which is also divine and holds all things together."

"Yes but there is one great difference," Numer explained. "The Christian Logos or Eternal Word knows and wills what he does in creation. He does not act through necessity, as the Stoics say of their Logos. He exercised his supreme freedom in becoming a man, taking our nature to himself, and redeeming us."

"Redeeming us from what?" Marcus asked, a little puzzled.

"From the evil and darkness inside which all humans have, and which the Christians call sin. It includes the evils of pride, anger, laziness, and lust."

Marcus thought about that for a moment; most of the mystery religions that he knew also promised some kind of salvation, but they did not involve any kind of personal effort or conversion. This was new.

But he had another question. "You mentioned the twelve sent by Jesus to teach the world, whom he called apostles. Did you ever meet any of them?"

"No," Numer shook his head rather sadly, "I'm too young. The last surviving apostle, John, who wrote the most about the Logos, died at the beginning of Trajan's reign, near Ephesus, a few years before I was born. But my uncle—my mother's brother—actually met him and received instruction in the Christian faith from him."

"Is that how you became a Christian?"

"Yes. My father and mother were horrified that I was becoming a Christian. But my uncle was such a kind man, and was so clear in his teachings and convictions, that I was convinced. I have never seen another man so courageous, especially at the hour of his death."

* John 1: 1, 3.

"How did he die?" Marcus asked

"I would prefer not to talk about it," Numer said with emotion in his voice. "Let me just say that he was a Christian, and that he paid the ultimate penalty about twelve years ago. I was around eighteen at the time; his courage changed my life."

Seeing how moved Numer had become, Marcus felt uncomfortable. He thought it much safer to ask more about the Logos or Word.

"But getting back to the Logos, explain again how it can be that if Jesus comes from the Father, he is not inferior to the Father."

"There is a great deal of controversy about this question right now in Alexandria. One of the Gnostic philosophers, Basilides, has connected the Christian idea of the Logos with a complex system of subordinate beings that come from the One, an idea proposed by the Neo-Platonists. According to him, Christ, or the Logos, belongs to an inferior world of eons, and is not really divine or eternal. Lots of Christians have been fooled by this kind of thinking, since it seems more sophisticated than the simple generation described in the Gospel. Basilides also has many kinds of mystical numbers and ceremonies in his philosophical system . . . but it is not the truth that we received from the apostles. My uncle was very clear to me about this. He had gotten into a public argument with Basilides about it once; but Basilides had too many supporters, and my uncle was driven out of the room."

"It seems that Christians have their intellectual divisions, too," Marcus said, a little self-complacently.

"It's no surprise. Christ himself had predicted that many would speak in his name and try to deceive his followers, and Paul, one of his early followers, had to fight all his life against falsifiers of Christ's teachings. To be frank about it, Marcus, we don't have all the vocabulary yet to explain Christ's teachings philosophically. My friend Justin and others are still trying to work it out. It will probably take centuries. But the best answer now is that, without ceasing to be God, God became a human being in the Word, in the Logos himself."

Marcus remembered his conversations with Junia about this . . . and how he had rejected her argument. But now he was beginning to see things more clearly. Numer was making a connection with the philosophy he knew. The Logos is the Word of the Father, his perfect Image, the Almighty One . . . who became a man for us and died on the cross.

"But why did he have to die on the cross? It's a shameful way to die, reserved for criminals and slaves."

"For two reasons, Marcus, to redeem us from sin through his sacrifice, through the voluntary offering of his blood, and to make it possible for us to share in his divine life when he rose from the dead. In a word, he did all of this because he *loved* us."

There was that word again, which Christians so often spoke of. Marcus wondered: *Would he ever understand it?* But it seemed to be the key to the whole mystery of how and why the divine Logos became a man.

XIV.

On a small island in the Tiber river stood a makeshift hospital for sick and worn-out slaves who had been rejected by their masters. In earlier times there had been a Temple of Aesculapius on the site—Aesculapius, the god of medicine and healing. Marcus had heard of it, but he had no desire to go near it, or to see people who lived there in such miserable conditions. He even felt sorry for those who had been ordered by Caesar's government to take care of them. So he was much surprised when, only three weeks after he had started to learn about Christianity, Numer and Dédicus asked him to visit the hospital with them.

"Master Marcus," Numer said, as if teasing him, "are you ready to see a little human misery?"

Being a Patrician, Marcus had always been sheltered from human suffering. He knew that people suffered, but it never occurred to him that he could or should do something about it. He thought himself quite a hero for choosing never to ride on the litter—unlike the rest of his family. He often walked in the busy Roman streets among the crowds, often in a simple tunic.

He tried to make an excuse. "But why should I go, Numer? I'm just beginning to learn about Christianity."

"Well, this is one of the better ways to learn more about it," Numer answered, "for Christ had a great love for the poor and needy. He even identified himself with them when he said that 'as you did it to one of the least of these my brethren, you did it to me.'" *

"Very well," said Marcus, as if he were going to do something very brave because he deeply disliked doing it. "And what do you have in your hand, Numer?"

"A basket of figs and dates . . . Cyprian dates!"

"Cyprian dates! Why, they're only for the rich; my sister used to love them."

"Yes, Marcus, they're only for the rich, and that's precisely why we're going to bring them to the very poor."

When they reached the island, they entered a large, rather ugly stone building near the shore. Patients were lined up in rows on the floor, some on the bare stone directly, some with woolen mats beneath them. The odor was incredibly foul, and Marcus felt that he was going to vomit.

Numer took him firmly by the arm and said, "Don't worry. You'll get used to it. Come over here. There's a man who they say has not received a visitor in a long time." He pointed to an old slave with a scruffy white beard who was lying in a corner.

As Marcus approached him, the old man's eyes lit up expectantly. He was covered by a soiled brown cloak, and Marcus noted that underneath it he was naked. He was not

* Matthew 25: 40.

shivering, however, because of the heat from a stove in the middle of the room, and the many bodies around him.

Junia's brother, not knowing what to say or do, and feeling very awkward, simply asked him how he was doing . . . to which the old slave replied: "Not very well." His face was bloated, and when he moved his body, his face writhed with pain. Despite his ailments, he was grateful for the Cyprian dates and the flask of good wine that Marcus gave him. The old man ate two of the dates and put the rest in the corner next to his mat, as if to protect them.

He then told Marcus a little about his life. He was originally from Cappadocia.* He was sold into slavery during the time of Nerva, and he had worked for thirty years on the estate of a wealthy Equestrian, at a villa just outside of Rome. He had had some children and even grandchildren; but they had not come to visit him, though some of them had already bought their freedom and were living a good life in the City.

After he had spoken for a while, he asked Marcus who he was. Marcus looked away from him for a moment; he had been listening closely, and something very deep was stirring in him, but he could not name it. He could not bring himself to say that he was the son of Gaius Metellus Cimber, Consul of Rome. At that particular moment, such things hardly mattered.

"Just call me Marcus," he said simply. "I'm a Roman citizen."

"I'm very grateful to you, sir, for having listened to me and for the Cyprian dates. But why have you visited me? You do not even know me . . ."

Marcus—not usually at a loss for words—did not know what to say. He could have told him about how Dédicus had saved his life. He could have told him about his conversations with Numer, about his sister, Junia, who had died for Christ, about his father . . .

---

* Cappadocia was a Roman province, corresponding to the eastern part of present-day Turkey.

So he simply looked at the old man and took his hand into his own. "Why did I visit you? Because I wanted to." And after making sure that he was resting comfortably, and adjusting his mat for him, Marcus went to join Numer and Dédicus, who were visiting other patients.

XV.

As the weeks went by, Claudia was ever more disappointed as Marcus delayed deciding about their marriage . . . but she was finding a source of consolation in her servant, Cynthia. She had had other personal servants before, but none could match her for intelligence and responsibility. If it had to do with a social engagement or an appointment, Cynthia would always think ahead; and she had saved Claudia some embarrassing moments by reminding her of certain details or events. As to the arrangement of the house, Cynthia directed the servants without Claudia's needing to be involved. And the other servants respected her because she was clear with them, without being domineering.

But it was not only her efficiency that Claudia admired—though as a Roman that is what she most valued. There was an awareness, a sympathy in Cynthia's eyes that she had not seen in another servant, nor even in her father's or mother's eyes. It seemed to Claudia that Cynthia was making a good effort to understand her and to help her. She began to speak about her feelings to Cynthia, in a way that she would never do among her peers; with them she was always trying to appear nonchalant and in perfect control of herself.

"You know, Cynthia, I just don't want to fail in things," she confided to her one day. "It's a sign of weakness. That's why I so want to have Marcus as a husband."

Cynthia simply nodded and said nothing on that occasion lest she seem forward. But she did think and pray afterward about what Claudia had said, because Scintilla was advising her to bring more things to prayer, as she was coming closer to Christ and his Way. It seemed to her that the main reason why Claudia so much wanted to win at everything—including things connected with men and marriage—was to please her father. Publius was very intent on this marriage, for it could greatly enhance his stature. But she also noticed that Publius would frequently ridicule Claudia, and call her useless, even in the smallest things; this treatment would only make the daughter more determined to succeed, out of shame or rebellion.

One day, Cynthia found her mistress upset because Marcus had canceled a dinner appointment, saying he had to be with some friends to discuss an important issue of philosophy. After she had calmed down a bit and was alone in her chamber, Cynthia quietly knocked at the door.

"May I come in, Miss?"

"Yes of course," Claudia said, with an attentive look in her eyes and a friendly tone in her voice. Cynthia knew that, six months before, her mistress would not have used that tone with her. "What would you like?"

"I've been thinking about something you told me a week ago, Miss—about your not wanting to fail at things, and that for this reason you were upset with Master Marcus."

"Yes, that's true," Claudia answered, "but what are you trying to say?"

"It's only a thought, Miss," Cynthia said in a very delicate voice. "But could it be that what you really want to do is to please your father in all of this, because it means so much to him? Do you have such a sincere or deep affection for Master Marcus, that you would like him for a husband?"

Claudia's first thought was that Cynthia was mistaken, because she *did* feel some attraction to Marcus, despite his abstract and inconstant ways. But her servant's words affected her. She had not considered that her father could be such a motivator of her thoughts and actions; she had always conceived herself as very independent, as was the mentality of all rich young women those days—whether for choosing a husband or for reaching other goals in life. But perhaps her servant was right.

She looked back at Cynthia in a thoughtful way and said that she would consider what she had said, and added only: "You may leave me now."

———

About a week later, Claudia caught a bad cold after a dinner party and a day watching plays and games at the Circus Maximus. The weather had been chilly and the wind strong, and Cynthia had asked her to wear a hood and a warmer robe—but Claudia had refused, saying that she was warm enough with only her palla.*

The next day, Claudia became quite ill, with a fever, a headache, and a deep cough. Her father was quite busy those days and did not want to catch her illness, so he sent her a physician but did not visit with her himself. None of her friends came to visit her, either. Each passing day, she seemed more embittered by this neglect, and was becoming miserable and cross with those taking care of her.

Cynthia remembered Junia's illness, which had been similar to this, and the wonderful service that Marcia had given to her. She also recalled one of Scintilla's recent talks to her on charity; she was not think of herself, but of her mistress and her fellow servants. Certainly Claudia could have commanded her to attend her, but Cynthia had determined to do it for another reason. Somehow she would try to find Christ in Claudia, who seemed, however, very far from God.

Cynthia tried to anticipate her mistress's needs. She made sure that Claudia rested properly, and that she drank plenty of water—a Greek physician had once told her that water was a very effective remedy for colds. One day, with the

---

* A Roman woman's outer garment, corresponding to the man's toga.

permission of Publius, Cynthia hired a flautist to come and play several songs for the invalid. Another day, Cynthia read her some scenes from a play that she knew Claudia had enjoyed seeing. And as she was doing these things, she thought to herself, *This is exactly what Junia did for me when I was sick; I'm simply changing roles.*

Claudia was grateful. The day when Cynthia had read from the play and had brought her mistress the favorite pearl necklace, Claudia smiled at her from her bed—a generous smile that lit up her bright brown eyes. It was the first time that Claudia had ever smiled at a servant. As Cynthia was about to leave her so she could rest, she motioned for her to come closer. Leaning toward her, she said in a hoarse voice, "Thank you, Cynthia, for all that you're doing for me. And . . ." Here she hesitated, as if trying to find courage to continue. "I want you to know I'm very sorry I did not let you visit your father in his last days."

Cynthia bowed deeply to her mistress as she left the room. Tears were welling up in her eyes, though she didn't want them to. Her body was trembling as she gave thanks to Christ for the miracle.

The next day, Scintilla, who had been praying for her and Claudia for several months, heard the story, as did Frieda, a young slave woman from Germany—about Cynthia's age—with blonde hair, fair skin, and blue eyes, who had run away from a brothel near the Temple of Isis just a few months before. Like Cynthia, Frieda was learning about Christ; and Cynthia was helping her to learn Latin, and to read and write.

XVI.

As Marcus was meeting with Numer on the Aventine Hill, Justus and Discalus were becoming good friends. Sometimes Discalus would come with his son, Gaius, for dinner at Justus's house on the road to Ostia, and Justus likewise would visit with Discalus at his fishstand on the Via

Bibertica near the Fishermen's Forum. Sometimes they would joke about their childhood days, growing up in northeastern Latium, though they were from different villages, and other times about how each of them had come to be in the fish business. Justus was also becoming friends with other shopkeepers in Rome, and to one, a carpenter with a lathe on the same street as Discalus, he had even begun to speak about Christ.

One day, as Justus and Discalus were walking in a park near the Baths of Neptune in the early afternoon, Discalus began to speak of his deceased wife, Drusilla.

"She was one of the best women you could imagine, Justus. She was from Umbria* originally, and was related to one of my father's in-laws. She was a farm girl, and never stopped being one, despite years in Rome. She was a very sincere person, with an abundance of common sense, and a kind of country shrewdness about things. You would have enjoyed meeting her."

"I'm sure. But tell me, did she like Rome?"

"At first she didn't, but she put up with it because she knew I wanted to make a living here. She did make some good friends with the wives of other shopkeepers, but I could tell she always yearned to go back to Umbria . . . to the hills and farmlands. But . . . she never complained, and I'm sure it was because she loved me very much . . ."—and here Discalus's voice began to break, and his eyes moistened. "Gaius just adored her."

They sat down for a moment on a white marble bench near one of the public waterways that Hadrian had constructed ten years earlier; a colorful bust of him stood just a few paces away from where they were sitting. Justus hoped to hear more about Drusilla but, given Discalus's emotion, thought it best just to sit silently. In a moment Discalus continued to speak.

* A farming region of central Italy, northeast of Latium, the region of the Alban Hills where Rome is located.

"She died in a fire on our street. You know how the *insulae** can be very dangerous, especially at night. I suspect that someone on the second floor did not properly put out a lantern, though I never found out for sure. We heard cries in the middle of the night, which woke us up. We got out of bed, woke up Gaius, and began to run toward the stairs, which were partially on fire. I was carrying little Gaius, and, as I felt my way down the stairs, I looked back to make sure that Drusilla was coming behind us . . . it was hard to see through the smoke, but I thought she was. But . . ."—and here his voice began to choke up again . . . —"it was . . . it was someone from an upper floor who looked like her. When we got outside, I realized my terrible mistake. She must have fallen and hit her head, or maybe the smoke overwhelmed her."

Justus shook his head slowly, and said a silent prayer to Christ for Drusilla. "I'm sorry," was all he could say.

"Little Gaius was only six years old, but he wanted to go back into the flames to get her. I didn't let him. It would have been death for him too. All this happened three years ago last January. I've not forgiven myself for what happened, and I've never forgiven the gods for what they did to me."

Justus again paused for a moment. "Tell me, Discalus" he said in a quiet voice, "have you ever thought of remarrying? Maybe it would take away some of your loneliness, and you could give Gaius a mother . . ." His voice trailed off at that.

Discalus lightly touched Justus's knee in appreciation for his thought. "Thank you, Justus, but I can never find another like her; and Gaius knows that, too. At times, when I take a break or after I close the shop, I just walk about the streets, feeling very lonely, as you say. I don't want to go to one of the brothels; that would be betraying Drusilla. Gaius is my only consolation. I know I'm too harsh with him at times, and I hit him for no reason."

* Literally "islands," but referring to the blocks of tenement houses in which most of Rome's inhabitants lived. Some of them grew to be four and five stories high; they were very prone to fires because they were made of wood

Justus just shook his head slowly and prayed for his friend. Soon he would *have* to speak with him about Christ, and the immense peace and joy that Christ could bring him if he could believe in him. He thought of the words that he and his family had just read after dinner that day from Matthew's Gospel, which one of the priests had lent him: "Come to me, all you who labor and are heavily burdened, and I will give you rest." * He yearned to give his friend Discalus a share of that rest, but he sensed that now was not the time.

XVII.

Marcus kept seeing Numer and Atticus regularly. More and more he was understanding the truth and intellectual depth of the Christian Logos. He was also comprehending more about the mystery of the Hebrew people, whom he had always considered backward and fanatical. They had a series of writings that had predicted the coming of a Messiah, who would be their King, as well as their savior. To demonstrate the meaning of the Hebrew prophecies more clearly, Numer had given him a copy of a Dialogue that his friend Justin was writing, based on a debate he had had with a Jew named Trypho in Ephesus. Reading the carefully reasoned words, Marcus could see how the Logos not only fulfilled the Hebrew prophecies, but truly summed up their whole history. What a tragedy that their leaders had rejected him . . .

From his first conversations with Dédicus, and then with Numer, Marcus was discovering that the Christian Logos fulfilled some of the great insights of the philosophers he had been studying for four years. The Christian Son of God was eternal, just as eternal as Plato's world of ideas was . . . and this Son was himself without change, as Parmenides had conceived of being. Yet without ceasing to be change-

---

* See Matthew II: 28.

less, he became a human being, with the combination of act and potency that all earthly things have, according to Aristotle. What is more, the words of the Logos would endure forever, just as long as the *logos* of Heraclitus and the Stoics . . . for Christ had said, "Heaven and earth will pass away, but my words will not pass away." *

It seemed amazing to Marcus that he was each day stepping into a beautiful new world of thought and speculation. As he walked up to the Aventine house, his mind was racing with many questions to ask Numer; but when he met him, the Alexandrian surprised him.

"Marcus," he said, as soon as he had walked into the courtyard, "let's go to the baths ** today." That was just like Numer, Marcus reflected. He was bright, well informed, but had an unpredictable and charming side that never ceased to entertain. He reminded Marcus of Junia's friend Marcia.

Marcus had not gone to the baths for the several months when he was meeting with Numer and Atticus. But today, as it was warm, he was happy to postpone his questions and go along. His interest increased when he was told that Dédicus was going to meet them there.

They were going to the Baths of Trajan, which were more up to date than the Baths of Neptune; they also had a very ample gymnasium. After they had gone to the dressing room and put on some leather trunks, Numer, as usual, came up with a novel idea: "Let's skip the tepidarium today—who wants to be tepid, anyway? And as for the caldarium—we can just as well perspire in the gymnasium and get exercise too. I challenge you both to a wrestling match and a tough game of trigon, since we are three."

---

* Luke 21: 33.
** Large, very decorative buildings, with marble floors and mosaics, where Romans refreshed themselves, usually near midday, before the main meal. The full procedure was to go first to the tepidarium, with lukewarm water, then to the caldarium, with hot water, and then, after an anointing and drying up perspiration, into the frigidarium, or cold-water pool.

Both Marcus and Dédicus laughed. "*Optima propositio*" (great idea), they said. Marcus was quite happy with Numer's idea of skipping the tepidarium. Over the years, many things he had seen happening there had disgusted him. In one tepidarium, at the Baths of Neptune, he had seen one of the Emperor's guards making love with one of his mistresses in the view of all the other men there.* He had also seen many wealthy Romans there with their smooth-skinned boy slaves, playing with them sexually in one corner of the baths reserved for that purpose. Marcus could never approve their behavior; he considered it to be contrary to the law of nature, as he and his father had often discussed.

As they entered the gymnasium—a large room with its walls decorated by colorful green and red mosaics of athletes boxing, wrestling, and throwing a discus—they first warmed up by running a bit and stretching their arms and legs. They began playing trigon, a vigorous game of catch; Dédicus, tallest of the three and with the best aim, won all three games they played . . . though Numer almost won the third game. "Dédicus," Numer said, "where did you learn to throw so well?" With a rather grim but truthful humor, Dédicus replied, "It's from throwing all those stones at the Roman soldiers occupying Palestine." And both Numer and Marcus laughed heartily, though they knew well that for Dédicus what he said was not a joke.

After that, they paired up for a wrestling match. From the time he was ten years old, Marcus had received lessons from one of the well-known wrestlers in Rome. His father loved the sport, and had been a champion in his youth, during the reign of Domitian.** Marcus was well-built and had taken easily to it, being able to best most of his classmates at it. Dédicus proved fairly easy to defeat, though Marcus had

* There were separate baths for men and women, though in later, decadent days the baths became mixed.
** Domitian, a fierce persecutor of Christians, was the first emperor to deify himself during his lifetime. He reigned from A.D. 81 to 96.

some compunction about pinning to the ground the man who had saved his life some months before. Marcus won all three matches, but Numer was different. He had obviously been observing Marcus and had learned some things to do and not to do. The first time, Marcus pinned him with relative ease. The second time was different, for Numer was learning quickly. The third time, Numer actually pinned Marcus—with a combination of strength and cleverness. He smiled afterward to Marcus, with his teeth sparkling brightly in the middle of his dark face, and the whites of his eyes shining with competition. "Next time, Marcus, I'll get you."

"Now wait a minute," Marcus said good-naturedly. "Atticus once told me that Christ said Christians should turn the other cheek."

"Well," Numer answered quickly, "I think he wasn't speaking about wrestling."

After they had trained a bit more, and were perspiring profusely, they went to the anointing room, where they dried their skins and put some ointment on their bodies. Then they went directly to the frigidarium and jumped into the cold water. It was an exhilarating feeling. Marcus had never had such an enjoyable time at sports in his life.

On the way back to Aventine, Dédicus, who had to present a study the next day at the Athenaeum, said his good-bye, and Marcus took advantage of his time alone with Numer to ask some direct questions. But this time his questions were not theoretical or philosophical . . . they were far more personal.

"But tell me more about the other fellows at the house. They all seem to be very excellent and manly, but they never speak about women. I have yet to see a woman at your house."

"Oh, some women do come to the house at times—for instance when we celebrate the Sunday Eucharist just before dawn. They come with their families. Someday, when you are more than an inquirer into the Faith, and become a catechumen, I'll invite you."

"Good," said Marcus, pursuing his point. "But it seems to me that neither you, nor Dédicus, nor any of those fellows is interested in marrying. Is that true?"

Numer stopped short and looked at Marcus directly. "Yes, it's true; we're not looking to marry."

"Is it that you're going after the pearl of great price—or the hundredfold—that Christ spoke about?"

Numer was surprised at how quickly Marcus was picking up things. "Where did you learn that expression, Marcus?"

"From Atticus. He's telling me everything that Christ said and did. We're now covering his public ministry, and he told me that one of his most powerful sayings was that 'he who gives up wife and children and lands for my sake, will receive a hundredfold in this life, and life everlasting.' Now tell me, Numer, is that what all of you are doing?"

"Yes, Marcus," the North African said simply; "sooner or later you should know. That's exactly what we're doing. We're trying to imitate the first apostles of Christ; they gave up everything in order to follow him. It's the pearl of great price."

"But, Numer," Marcus protested. "That's beyond human power to do! Not even the gods can give up sexual relations."

"Well, Marcus, that's why they're false gods. If you really believed, if you really loved Christ, who never married, he would give you the strength to do it. *We're* doing it and succeeding, with Christ's help and the help of his virgin Mother."

Marcus shook his head; he could not understand it, but he was discovering many things about Christianity that he could not understand.

By then they had reached the courtyard of the estate, with the clear pool of water surrounded by poplar trees. Marcus invited his friend to sit with him on one of the marble benches near the entrance.

"One more thing, Numer. You and these fellows live here in Rome and go about your ordinary activities, don't you? I know that Aulus is an attorney, Atticus is an architect, and you and Dédicus are philosophy students. Aren't you afraid to show your faces in public? I'm sure you see that anybody could denounce you at any time, as they did my sister. You could be crucified, or thrown to the lions. And yet you all seem so joyful all of the time, as if you don't care."

"As to being in the world, we're *supposed* to be there," Numer answered simply, "because the Lord Christ said to his disciples, 'You are the light of the world; you are the salt of the earth.' We can't run from the world, even if it's corrupt. We have to redeem the world, and bring people to Christ."

"But that's impossible. How can you save a world that does not want to be saved? Who really wants to hear about prayer, sacrifice, or chastity? Listen—please excuse me for putting it so bluntly. I do like you all very much, and you're the best men I have ever known—even better than my father, in many ways—but I think you're all crazy."

"You're right, Marcus; we are crazy," Numer said. "We're crazy for the love of Jesus Christ."

DECISION

XVIII.

After his conversation with Numer, Marcus did not go home right away to his father's estate on the Esquiline Hill. Something was requiring an answer from him. He had to find a quiet place so he could think. He went to the same park where Justus and Discalus had spoken a few weeks before, next to the pond with the full-sized statue of Hadrian. It was the dinner hour, and most people were now at home; a few small birds were flying here and there among the trees beside the water . . .

The last year had been amazing to him. It had begun a few months after Junia's death, when Dédicus rescued him from death on the street leading to the old Forum. In addition, all that he had heard about the Logos from the Christians had fascinated him—that it is not an impersonal force directing the cosmos, as the Stoics taught and his father believed, but that the Logos is really the only-begotten Son of the Father with such a love for mankind that he became a man, and brought eternal life to us through his own life and death; and what is more, that this Word is truly the summary and culmination of all the philosophers' theories beforehand, and of all of the Hebrew Scriptures, as well! He still was struggling with it all, trying to analyze it and give it some kind of definition—but then he could hear his sister teasing him again: "Oh, Marcus, you're always trying to define things! Let's just say that he's God and that He loves me very much."

He was experiencing a greater understanding, but also something more. There was something about Numer's faith and joy, and the cheerfulness of the young men at the Aventine house, which deeply attracted him. They were

Christians, they could be denounced at any time—yet they were happy and carefree, and they knew how to help one another. Thinking back, Marcus recognized in them the same sort of spirit that Marcia had, though at the time it had seemed to him to be silliness. Now he saw that their happiness had deep roots, though he still could not quite understand it.

But then again, why should he try to understand or control everything? He wanted the same joy they had, wherever it came from.

And they were all normal men, like himself, attracted to women—and yet giving up marriage and physical relations with women for the sake of something greater. It was astounding to him. They had truly given up everything for the dead Galilean, who they claimed was really alive. They were "crazy" for the love of Jesus Christ, as Numer had just told him.

And then, unexplainedly, as if a small flicker of fire kindled in his soul, Marcus imagined that someday he might be able to be crazy, too.

He thought again about his visit to the hospital on the Isla Tiberina with Dédicus and Numer. *Was that really I who did that?* Marcus asked himself, and smiled. To speak with a slave in such a way, to try to console him, to bring him food and wine, to listen patiently to his sad story? But then he remembered how Atticus had given him Christ's own words shortly after they made the visit: "For I was hungry, and you gave me to eat; sick, and you visited me." Numer had tricked him into doing it, but now he recognized it as a a great favor.

Strolling around the pond, he came to the same stone bench where Justus and Discalus had spoken. *What can I say to all of this?* he asked himself as he sat down for a few moments, looking at the sky and not thinking about anything in particular. Then he got up and walked back around the pond, where he happened to see the reflection of his face in the water. The curly brown hair, the light blue eyes, the inquiring look on his face—a face looking back at him. *What I'm really experiencing is love,* Marcus told himself, *that mysterious thing that I've only read about before. Yes, for the past nine months I've been greatly loved, and now I must somehow say yes to it.*

He had decided. He would ask to be accepted as a catechumen, no longer an inquirer. And also—and here he winced and clasped his hands nervously—he would have to break off with Claudia, and give his father a good reason. It would be very hard. As he walked toward home, for the first time he found himself actually praying to the Christian God: "O Jesus, the Eternal Logos, give me the words, give me the strength."

XIX.

Gaius had been working particularly long hours those days. The other Consul was a very elderly man and a great favorite of the Emperor, so Gaius was forced to do a great deal of his work, as well as his own. It was hard for him to continue in his calm, self-possessed way, as he had been able to do as a senator. He found himself becoming more and more irritable, giving in to his lower emotions, which, as a professed Stoic, he was supposed to suppress.

He had been particularly irritated by Marcus, who had delayed for months giving him a decision about Claudia, the wife he had chosen for him. Despite his insistence, Marcus had been putting him off. So he was greatly interested when Marcus asked to see him one day in his study. He had just dismissed his *clientes*, and was preparing a speech that he was to present in the Senate next day.

Marcus appeared wearing his toga with the Curian purple stripe; he wanted to be as respectful as possible with his father. He had anointed his forehead, and even had had his beard curled a bit, as was the latest fashion among young men. He bowed slightly as he entered the room, recognizing not only one of the Consuls of Rome, but his father, the *paterfamilias*. Though Marcus had reached the age of majority—he was twenty-two—he was still living in his father's house and owed him obedience.

"Father," Marcus began, "I have something important, though painful, to tell you."

Gaius sat upright and looked into his son's eyes. He had been noticing something different about him in recent months; he was more alert, less dreamy in his ways. He also seemed to be dressing a little more neatly, and was more cheerful about things. This change in his son had actually annoyed Gaius somewhat, since he was still suffering from a deep depression, though he didn't want to admit it, after the death of his daughter. She had been his favorite always.

"Speak, my son," said Gaius. "Get to the point."

"As you know, Father, I have always had a great love for ideas and books. I have made it my work in the last four years."

Gaius nodded gravely; he had desired a more active, political life for his son . . .

"Well," Marcus continued, "over the last few months I have discovered a new philosophical system—related to the idea of the logos—that comes from the East. It has attracted my attention greatly. I need at least another year to see if it is truly for me, and to study it more deeply."

"And what is this system? Does it have a name?"

Marcus was prepared for that question. He couldn't tell his father that he was interested in Christianity, but he didn't want to lie, either.

"It's rather new, Father, and somewhat controversial, but I'm very interested in it. To investigate it further, I may need to travel to Ephesus or Alexandria."

"And what does this mean as far as your marriage with Claudia is concerned?" Gaius asked him directly, as he rose from his seat.

"I cannot bind her to any commitment, Father; out of fairness, I release her to look for another."

"Then this new philosophy is more important to you than your marriage?"

"Yes, Father," Marcus answered directly, "at least for now. Even if I were to marry, my mind would not be in it."

Gaius walked to the corner of his study, and lightly touched the head of a bust of Cicero that had stood there for years. Then he walked toward the atrium, with his hands behind his back. He was thinking. After a couple of moments, he returned to his son.

"Very well. Let another year go by. By then you will be twenty three years old. You should have married four years ago. But by the end of that time, I will expect you to marry the woman I choose for you."

Marcus bowed to him, but said nothing. He was not ready to agree to his father's plans for him, but thought it best not to oppose him now.

On his way to his room, he noticed his mother, Aurelia, walking on the far side of the atrium. Since Junia's death, she had become more serious and thoughtful. She had also gotten closer to her husband, and took more interest in his career. Though she was always a fashionable person, it seemed to Marcus that she was not as concerned about games or dinner parties as she had been. She also listened more carefully to others. He was about to go up to her and tell her about his conversation with his father, but then he thought it best to let Gaius tell her.

XX.

When Claudia heard that Marcus was canceling their engagement, she was furious. She felt it an insult to herself and to her family, especially her father. For months she had done practically everything she could to win him, and had even begun to feel an attraction to him . . . and to imagine herself as his wife. Now she felt nothing but hatred and resentment toward him, and began to think of some kind of revenge.

Since she and her servant, Cynthia, had become friends, she confided her feelings almost immediately to her. She felt she could be more open to her than with her peers, and knew from experience now that Cynthia would give her sound advice. Cynthia had actually suspected that Marcus might break off the engagement, as Scintilla had told her that Marcus was visiting Numer and his friends and that already some Christian families in the City were praying for him to discover the Way of Christ.

"Miss," she asked Claudia, "what reason did he give for canceling the engagement?"

"Oh," Claudia said angrily as she rolled her eyes and waved her hand, "something about a new philosophy that he wants to study, and that it would take up all of his time for the next year."

"I suppose," said Cynthia gently, "that it is his right to decide this, as a free citizen of Rome, for he had made no formal engagement with you."

"I don't deny that it is his right," Claudia said impatiently. "But he has constantly hurt my feelings—and I have put out so much effort to win him. You know that, Cynthia. You've been part of it. I feel like strangling him."

Cynthia was silent for a moment, as she reflected. She took Claudia's hand in hers—something that now seemed very natural to them both—and said to her softly: "Miss, I think this is perhaps a gift from the gods; they don't want you to make a big mistake."

"What do you mean?"

"Marcus," Cynthia answered simply, "is so unlike you, with all of his books and theories. I think you would not have anything to talk about. You wouldn't enjoy his company for long."

In one sense, that objection did not matter to Claudia, or

to her father; marriage was more a political convenience for them, as it was for many wealthy families in Rome. Claudia had thought little about their compatibility. But she could see the wisdom of Cynthia's words; she was speaking of a nobler view of marriage, which did have a certain appeal to her. She knew that Cynthia had her good in mind.

"What you say could be true, Cynthia. But that doesn't change my situation. I've wasted seven months of my life waiting for him. I'm almost twenty years old now; soon I'll be too old to marry. Nobody will want me." *

"Miss," said Cynthia softly, "I know someone who might interest you more. He's strong and good looking, he's very practical, and he's a man of virtue."

"You've described an impossibility in the Rome of our times. Who is he?"

"His name is Quintus, and he's a captain in the Praetorian Guard."

"Quintus? He was the one so much in love with Junia, and was expected to marry her. Livia and I were both crazy about him. What is he doing now?"

"It took him a while to get over her death, but he's looking for a wife now."

"How could I meet him?" Claudia said with immediate interest.

"I can introduce him to you. He remembers me well, from the times he visited Junia, and he always respected me, though I was a slave. I can tell him about you."

Claudia paused for a moment, thinking about this new possibility. The Praetorian Guards had great prestige in Rome, and were very close to the Emperor. It would be almost as good a match as the son of a Consul. "Yes, dear Cynthia, yes. Make the arrangement," she said, and then she gave her servant an embrace, kissing her on the cheek. "You're the best purchase we've ever made."

* Roman women typically married between 14 and 18 years of age.

As she was leaving Claudia's room, Cynthia thought to herself, *If only you knew to whom I really belong, dear Mistress.* For she was soon to be baptized, at the Easter Vigil of the following year. And she had heard that Quintus had become a good friend of Septimus, who also was a member of the Praetorian Guard, and a Christian. She would somehow get word to Quintus about Claudia, and arrange for them to meet.

XXI.

In the eighteen months after Junia's death, Quintus had risen to the rank of Prefect of the Praetorian Guards. He had direct command of a division of soldiers, and personal access to the Emperor himself. But the months immediately following Junia's execution had been very hard for him. He had never met any other woman so lovely and intelligent, with the virtues of those women who had made Rome great in the days of the old Republic.

At one point he had thought of approaching her servant Cynthia as a possible bride, though she would have to become a freed woman first.* He had gotten to know her fairly well in his visits to Junia; he had always been impressed by the servant girl's common sense and native intelligence. Her smooth dark hair and good figure had also attracted him, but in the end he decided to search for someone else, especially after his promotion. He rejected the idea of taking her for a mistress, not only because it would be against the personal standards he had set for himself, but also because he knew it would not be worthy of her or of Junia. It would be more advantageous for him to marry someone of his own rank. His friends and relatives had advised him so.

For this reason he was most interested when he received a letter from Cynthia that spoke of a young woman named Claudia, daughter of Publius. The letter explained that she

---

* A Roman citizen could not marry a slave woman.

was originally intended for Marcus, but that Marcus had wanted to pursue a philosophical project for a year and had stopped seeing her. *Just like Marcus*, Quintus thought, *lost in his world of books again. But one man's loss can be another man's gain.* He had met Claudia on several occasions before, and had been impressed by her sharp practical mind and good looks. She was the type of person who could get things done, and that quality pleased his military mind. It was also rumored that her father could be elected a senator soon. The only disadvantage that he could think of was that she was a close friend of Livia, whom he despised. So he wrote back to Cynthia, asking her to arrange a meeting between Claudia and himself at her home.

Their first meeting went very well. There was a directness and honesty about Claudia that Quintus liked, and she did not engage in all the gossip or silliness that characterized other high-born women he had met. In this way she was quite unlike Livia and Livia's mother, Agrippina.

After Quintus left the dining room, while the servants were removing the platters and goblets from the table, Claudia found Cynthia, who was sewing a torn piece of clothing in her room. "Cynthia," she said, her eyes alight with excitement, "he's wonderful! He's strong, handsome, with such common sense. I feel much more at ease with him than with Marcus. You were right." And she gave her servant a big embrace, and kissed her on both cheeks, like a sister. But Cynthia was giving thanks in her spirit to Marcia and Junia, to whom she had been praying that things would work out well.

Because the Emperor was sending him soon to northern Gaul on a special mission for several months, Quintus decided to put off marriage until early in the following year; but after a few weeks he made a formal engagement, so that Claudia and her father would clearly know his intentions.

XXII.

As a family, Justus, Constantia, and their two children used to go to the house of Diodorus, where the Eucharist was held; there they had met Marcia and Scintilla. Usually the Mass was said by Cartos, Diodorus' brother, who had been ordained in Corinth by one of the bishops that Paul himself had ordained. But occasionally the bishop of the Church in Rome himself had offered the sacrifice, and such occasions had been times of great joy for the whole family.

But after Diodorus's death in the arena with his daughter, his house had been taken over by Caesar's praetors, so now they had had to go to different houses each Sunday. They would have to sing their hymns in soft voices, so that nothing could be heard from the street. And they would try to arrive at different times for the same service, so as not to attract attention. Once in a while, the Eucharist service was held in the catacombs, especially near the anniversary of a saint's death. It was at just such a service that they had met Junia for the first time, when they gave her a ride back to her home on the fish wagon.

Justus and Constantia wanted to have as many children as God wanted, but he had limited them to two. They gave thanks to him for their fine children, who were living the Faith well. Timotheus was hoping to become an attorney someday, and Carmina loved poetry and music. But still the parents wanted to have more children, to add more Christians to Christ's kingdom, and to spread his truth and love to the whole world. So at every Eucharist that they attended, they prayed for another child.

One night, Justus returned quite late from Rome. He had just delivered a large catch of fish to some shopkeepers along the Via Tiberatica. On such nights, Constantia usually went to bed earlier, leaving the olive oil lantern lit near the front entrance. But this time Justus was surprised to see that she was still up and waiting for him.

"Is there something wrong, Consti?" he asked.

"Oh, nothing is wrong," she said, with a very contented look in her eyes. "Everything is right."

"What do you mean?"

"Justus, for the last few days I have felt another life within me. Today I have known it for sure."

"Do you mean, Consti, do you mean . . . ?" he said as he grasped her right hand excitedly. "That it's a child? At last a child, as we've been praying for?"

"Yes, Justus, a child."

And Justus embraced his wife tenderly, as both of them said a prayer of thanksgiving to Jesus the Good Shepherd and his holy Mother.

XXIII.

Marcus now seriously began his entrance into the Faith. He started to read more carefully the Gospel accounts that Numer and Atticus had given him, along with certain letters of the Apostle Paul, especially to the Romans and the Corinthians. He was most struck by a passage from the first of Paul's letters to the Corinthians, toward the beginning: "For the doctrine of the cross is foolishness to those who perish, but to those who are saved, that is, to us, it is the power of God. . . . Where is the 'wise man'? Where is the scribe? Where is the disputant of this world? Has not God turned the 'wisdom' of this world to foolishness?" *

The foolish things, Marcus reflected. Dédicus's flinging himself before a wild chariot to save someone he didn't even know; his sister's visit to a slave, Cynthia's father, which became the talk of Rome the year before; his own visit to that slave on Tiber Island. If that visit ever became public, it also would become the talk of the town. And the most foolish of all, Christ's own ignominious death on the cross,

* See 1 Corinthians 1: 18, 20–21.

the most shameful way to die in the Roman Empire. *That is the true power of this movement*, he reflected. *Christianity has profound ideas, it is true . . . but there is something much greater behind it than an idea.*

Though Atticus had given him some hint about it previously, Marcus began on his own to look for friends whom he could interest in the message of Christ, just as Dédicus had done for him. Marcus was a childhood friend of Servianus, Livia's older brother; they were about the same age. Servianus was a fairly slight man, who had large luminous eyes and shared Marcus's interest in philosophy. Since the time they had entered the Athenaeum, in the same year, they had had many lively conversations together, often over a few glasses of posca wine in one of the cheaper taverns near the old Forum. Servianus had never mentioned anything directly to Marcus, but Marcus could tell that he was very sorry about what his mother and sister had done to Junia.

As a way of getting him to think about the ideals of Christianity, he gave Servianus some of the works of Philo, which showed the connection of Greek ideas with the Hebrew Scriptures and with the coming of the Messiah. From there, Marcus planned to speak with him more directly about the Logos, the Word of God, as the fulfillment of all philosophy. He was hopeful that this plan would lead Servianus closer to Christianity, at least intellectually.

Twice a week, Numer and Atticus invited Marcus to dinner at the Aventine House. He had been to the atrium before, but he had never been to the triclinum, where they took their meals. The room was fairly small, but on one wall was a large, colorful fresco of a spotted deer running over a green hilltop, and the sun rising just behind it. The floor was made of a very fine, polished green marble. Marcus was surprised at how neat and clean things were; because it was a residence of young men, many of them students, he had expected to see dust and disorder.

But he was most amazed at the quality of the food. It was not rich and luxurious, as had been served to him in Publius's triclinum, but it was tasty and wholesome. All the courses were there, beginning with some well-prepared eggs and leeks, then baked chicken and vegetables, and a dessert of apples and pears. There was also an attractive vase of field daisies and violets next to the tables where the men reclined to eat.

After they had sung a hymn and a brief prayer, Marcus asked Atticus if one of the fellows had prepared the meal.

"Oh, no," he said, "the women did."

"Women?" Marcus asked in surprise. "I thought this house was for men only."

"Yes it's true that only men live here. But there is a group of women, Christians like us, who take care of the house for us and prepare the meals sometimes. As you recall from our conversations, there was also a group of women who ministered to the Lord and his apostles. We are very blessed to have them, since we are not as worthy as the Lord and his apostles."

"But who are they? Can I meet them?"

"Well they prefer just to do their work and to leave. But you do know one of them already."

"Who?"

"Scintilla, who gave Junia lessons about the Lord and his teachings. She is the real leader of the group. And you'll be happy to hear that Cynthia is also a catechumen, and will be baptized this vigil of Easter by Telesphorus, bishop of Rome."

Everything now clicked in Marcus's mind. He had noticed that Cynthia had smiled at him, with a clever look on her face, during his visits to Claudia's house, as if she knew something that he did not. So this was the reason. And he had also noticed how Claudia and she were on very good terms, much closer than those typically seen between a Roman mistress and her servant. He said a brief prayer to the angels for her, so that she would find happiness in her life.

"In a way, I'm not surprised," Marcus answered Atticus. "She and Junia had become very close, especially in the last months of Junia's life."

"Yes," said Atticus, "and I guess we can see how Junia and Marcia keep working for their friends even now."

XXIV.

As the months went by, Gaius and Timotheus had become good friends. Though Timotheus was three years older, they liked to play hoops together in one of the parks near the Baths of Trajan, while their fathers were talking. At times, when Discalus and Gaius visited Justus's home, Timotheus would give rides to Gaius in the fish cart in the fields next to the road to Ostia, for Timotheus was old enough to handle the horse by himself. Gaius always wanted to steer it, though, and Timotheus would let him handle the reins sometimes.

With the honest simplicity of childhood, Timotheus told Gaius right away that his family were Christians, and that they sang a hymn to Christ the Savior every morning just before dawn, and at night before going to bed. On Sunday, the Resurrection day, they went to the Eucharist at a house on the Aventine Hill in Rome. Gaius had heard all kinds of insults and horrible stories about the Christians, including that they ate their own children, but with his child's good sense he had not believed them. His mother hadn't believed them, either. He remembered what his mother had told him once, after he asked a question about Christians: "Gaius, the Christians that I know here are very generous and hard working people. Other people just talk without knowing what they're saying, or they just repeat stupid rumors. I think some of them are jealous of the Christians because they have good families and happy children."

But neither she nor Gaius ever brought up the subject

with Discalus, because they knew that he was deeply anti-Christian, as were most of the shopkeepers on the Via Biberatica.

When Timotheus told his friend that he was a Christian, Gaius immediately told him that he wanted to be a Christian when he grew up. But Timotheus warned him what to expect. "It's pretty dangerous, Gaius. You know what happened to that woman Junia; my family knew her. But all her good looks and all her father's influence could not save her."

"I saw her just once, when she was in the chariot being led to the amphitheater. She was smiling at me. I think she was braver than a hundred Praetorian guards."

Timotheus laughed, but then he said. "And there are spies all around. You know that when families go to the Mass at the Aventine House, they have to go at different times, so as not to attract attention."

Gaius waved his hand and grinned. "That sounds neat, Timotheus. Sign me up as a Christian right away," he said as he gave his friend a little shove.

Both boys attended a school not far from Discalus's shop, which consisted of two fairly large rooms on the lower level of an apartment building. The older boys were in one room, the younger ones in the other. Constantia would normally drive her son the seven miles to the City in the fish cart each day, while Justus rested after his night trips from Ostia. Though she was five months pregnant, she did not mind the ride. The road was well traveled and smooth . . . and sometimes Carmina came with her. Often, in the mornings, she would stay in the City to shop and visit with the wives of some of the merchants. She had a good friend, Silvia, a woman in her middle twenties who had not married, and who ran a small poultry shop. Consti had already spoken with her several times about the teachings of Christ, and how much they had helped her in her life. To Consti's great joy, Silvia had become a catechumen a few weeks before.

At school the boys learned the basics of grammar, arithmetic, and use of the abacus for calculating, and how to read and write. In the higher grades the students read and copied from scrolls containing accounts of Caesar's Gallic wars, Cicero's orations, and Virgil's *Aeneid*. Occasionally they also read from the works of Terence and Plautus, though the Latin of these popular dramatists was becoming archaic by then. Each boy had a wax-coated tablet and a stylus.* Timotheus was one of the better students in the class, and some of the others were jealous of him, especially a group of them led by Odius, the son of a blacksmith who lived near Discalus's shop.

Classes let out at about the seventh hour of the day, for the boys to go back to their homes for lunch (*prandium*). Many were shopkeepers' and merchants' sons, and their fathers needed them to help with the afternoon business hours, which began around the tenth hour and lasted until sunset.

One day, in the month dedicated to Mars, the god of war, Odius, who was the same age as Timotheus, began to taunt him as they left the classroom. Timotheus was used to the taunting, and ordinarily would simply ignore it or brush it off in a lighthearted way; but today Odius was saying something different.

"Hey, Christian, dirty Christian!" he shouted. "Don't try to hide it—we know you're a Christian."

Timotheus turned around sharply and faced his antagonist. Odius was of medium height, well built for his age, with curly black hair and puffy cheeks; he was glaring at Timotheus with his tiny black eyes. Some other boys, part of his gang, began to say the same thing to Justus's son, adding a few other taunts: "A curse to you, Christian—you

* A pointed instrument used by the Romans to write on waxed tablets; similar to a present-day penknife.

77

worship a criminal! . . . Curse on you, Christian, enemy of the Emperor!"

After they had surrounded him and jeered at him, Odius pushed Timotheus to the ground, while another boy kicked him in the stomach. Timotheus managed to get up quickly and turned to face Odius, but just then Odius pulled out a small lead dagger from under his tunic; he had been hiding it there. He began brandishing it in front of Timotheus's face. Meanwhile several other boys began to surround him, menacing him with their sharp-pointed styluses—which they were supposed to have left in the classroom . . . and calling him "Christian, dirty Christian."

The younger boys came over to see what was happening, as they filed out from the other classroom. Gaius saw his friend surrounded by the older boys, with styluses in their hands. He hesitated for a moment, not knowing what to do . . . but then he began to walk toward them and to shout in his loudest voice: "Leave my friend alone, he never hurt you. Leave my friend alone!"

Odius glared at him and shouted back at him scornfully: "Get out of here, little mouse, if you know what's good for you. Are you a Christian too?"

But Gaius refused to leave. Instead he pushed himself through the circle of the older boys, and placed himself between Odius and Timotheus, looking his tormentor straight in the eyes. "Leave my friend alone," he said.

Odius was infuriated. With his left hand he smashed Gaius in the face, knocking him to the ground, and another older boy kicked him in the head until he was unconscious. When he saw what was happenng, Timotheus lurched toward the boy who was kicking Gaius, and knocked him to the ground. And at that moment Odius, more and more infuriated, stabbed Timotheus in the bottom part of his back with his dagger, and another boy who had a small dagger stabbed him in the upper part of his back. As he was staggering from these wounds, the other boys began to stab him also with their styluses, in the side and in the back. Timotheus fell to the ground, on top of Gaius in order to shield him from the others if he could.

The boys' teacher, whose name was Pontius and who was supposed to preserve order at the school, had watched the whole event and had done nothing. He had always suspected that Timotheus was a Christian, and one of his friends had told him that he had twice seen Justus and his family going to the Christian catacombs and that Justus had once spoken to him about Christ. So Pontius let his students taunt and bully Timotheus; but when they had began to stab him with their styluses, he intervened and sent them off to their homes. But he did nothing to help Timotheus, who was left bleeding in the street. He assumed that his own people would come and take care of him.

A crowd was gathering at the scene, but none of them did anything for Timotheus, who was unconscious and bleeding profusely; they only stared and asked each other what had happened. Gaius woke up and managed to wiggle himself free; his short white tunic was covered with his friend's blood. He ran to his father's shop, only three blocks away, and told Discalus what had happened, with so many words and with such intensity that Discalus could hardly understand him. Discalus ran to the scene and recognized Timotheus immediately, and sent Gaius for a doctor. One man from a shop nearby, a carpenter who knew Timotheus and liked him, brought a large container of hot water with fresh clean cloths. Discalus, muttering to himself and cursing all the gods at once, began to clean Timotheus's wounds on his back and sides. He had once been a physician's aid for the Roman army and knew how to clean and dress sword wounds fairly well.

Not long afterward, a doctor arrived, with some dressing linens, bandages, and ointment, along with a potion of water and mandrake roots. Timotheus was still breathing, but the doctor, an old grizzled man with deep furrows in his brow, examined him and had little hope for the boy. The stab wounds were multiple, and a couple of them were very near the heart. He did not want to move the boy, and asked the carpenter if he could provide some kind of shade against the sun and set up a barrier to keep away the people who were crowding around to see. One young man quipped as he walked by, "He looks like Julius Caesar, all covered with knife wounds." A few people laughed at that.

About a half hour later, Constantia and Carmina came in the fish cart in order to pick up Timotheus from school. Drawing near, they saw the crowd near the school entrance and immediately knew that something serious had happened. Constantia felt a deep sense of dread as she and her ten-year-old daughter made their way to the front of the scene. When she saw her son unconscious and bleeding on the street, she cried out and rushed to his side, and Carmina followed her. Seeing that he was already receiving medical attention, she knelt beside him and lightly caressed his face, passing her hand over his straight brown hair. She felt that she was going to faint, but she remained kneeling, thinking of Jesus' mother next to the cross. Carmina knelt next to her. Discalus and Gaius stood directly behind them, trying in some way to comfort them, but not knowing what to do.

"*O Jesu, Jesu Christe, salva nos,*" they heard Constantia say in a low mumur, and then they heard little Carmina add something that sounded like "*Virgo Maria.*"

Discalus had not heard of the *Virgo Maria*, but when he heard Constantia say *Jesu Christe* he knew that they must be Christians.

When he saw that Timotheus was being well attended, Discalus bent over and whispered to Consti that he would go back in the fish cart, and bring Justus. She nodded silently, as she kept passing her hand over her son's hair, her lips moving silently. When he arrived at the farm on the road to Ostia, he saw Justus behind the house, mending one of the wheels of the smaller cart. Justus looked surprised to see him, and smiled a broad welcome. But when Discalus told him what had happened at the school, his face became expressionless.

"Where is the boy now?" he asked in nearly a whisper.

"In front of the school building. A doctor is taking care of him, and the carpenter down the street has given an awning to protect him. Your wife and Carmina are with him, praying."

They ran to the well working fish cart, and Justus asked Discalus to drive. They said nothing as Discalus urged the horse to run faster. At first Justus seemed calm, but after the second mile or so he began to clench his fists and pound his forehead with his right fist. He was trembling, and saying something under his breath, which Discalus could not hear because of the clatter of the horse's hooves and the cart's wheels on the road.

He turned to Justus and said in a loud voice, "Justus, I know that you are Christians." And then he smiled at him. That smile calmed Justus down, and he looked back at his friend. "I'm glad that you know, Discalus," he said simply.

When they reached the scene of the stabbing, the crowd had mostly dissipated. Justus jumped from the cart immediately, letting Discalus find a place to leave it safely, along with the horse. Running to the school building, he saw Timotheus still lying on his stomach, though most of the bleeding had stopped. Constantia, looking very round in her pregnancy, was kneeling beside their son; she was whispering something in his ear. Little Gaius, who was about the same age as Carmina, was holding the girl's hand and trying to wipe away her tears with one of the extra linens that the carpenter had brought.

Justus let his wife know that he had arrived, and knelt down beside her to pray. After a minute or so, he felt someone's hand on his right shoulder. It was Discalus. He too had knelt down, and began to pray alongside him.

After a few minutes, the old physician, who had been taking care of the boy the whole time, got up slowly. When he was told that Justus was the boy's father, he went up to him with a relieved look on his face. He said, "It's amazing. There were six stab wounds, and two were very close to the heart. But I think he's going to recover. To which gods were you praying?"

XXV.

Dédicus also had been praying fervently for the last three months. Bishop Telesphorus had made the sign of the cross on his forehead and had anointed him, thus officially bringing him into the rank of the catechumens . . . .and he had been fasting regularly on Wednesdays and Fridays to prepare himself for the sacraments of initiation: Baptism, Confirmation, and Holy Communion.

His whole life had changed after he left Palestine, and after he met Titus at the Athenaeum; Titus had introduced him to Numer. He had learned not only of a Truth worth living and dying for, but of the importance of charity and forgiveness—which were so hard for him, after all the conflicts he had seen in Palestine with the hated Romans. But now, through God's grace, he had actually learned to pray for the Romans. And then there was that wild incident on the street near the old Forum, when he had been thinking about Christ's sacrifice for all men, and had thrown himself in the way of the charging chariot horses in order to save the life of a man he did not know—a man who turned out to be the son of a Roman consul. And now he had had the joy of seeing that same man coming closer to Christ as a catechumen.

Marcus was delighted for him, and he felt honored to be invited to the Easter Vigil service where both Dédicus and Cynthia were to be baptized. As a catechumen he had already attended several Masses. At one of them, he had learned that his good friend Atticus was a priest. Apparently he had been preparing for Holy Orders while studying architecture under Turibius. But he was very busy now, from what Marcus could see, giving classes, preaching, and administering Communion at various locations in Rome.

The Easter Vigil service was to be held at the home of a man named Justus, whom Marcus had never met. It was located somewhere on the road to Ostia, and was considered to be a safe location—many people would be attending, and there was less danger of their being seen or denounced to the imperial authorities. Marcus walked the distance with Numer and Dédicus, just as the sun was setting on a Saturday evening in early April. The house was fairly large, with a good portion of land around it, though it did not have a pond or courtyard in front of it. Marcus thought that it must belong to a plebeian who had made a good business for himself—perhaps a merchant of some sort. He could hear a couple of horses neighing in the field behind the house.

The Lord's sacrifice was to be held in the atrium; the main celebrant was the bishop of Rome himself, Telesphorus, a tall man with a thin, almost gaunt face—but with large bright eyes and a very gentle expression. *So*, Marcus reflected, *this is the successor of Peter, the Bishop of Rome, who presides over all the Churches*—of him he had heard much from Numer and Atticus. And then, not wanting to think it, he considered that there had to be a high price on the bishop's head in the City.

Justus and Constantia were welcoming the participants as they arrived at the front door, and Marcus noticed that she was pregnant, probably in her final weeks before giving birth. They had two children, a boy of about thirteen who seemed to Marcus to be prematurely old—he had a slight stoop, and at times had to steady himself by holding on to his father or putting his arm on the shoulder of his little sister, who stood next to him.

They took their places for the Easter Liturgy, and he took his place in the section reserved for the catechumens. He noticed in front of him a plebeian whom he had seen before, the owner of a fish shop on the Via Biberatica, which he had passed by many times; next to him stood a boy of about nine or ten years, whom he assumed to be the man's son. Another catechumen appeared to be an athlete or soldier. To his right was the section reserved for the women, all of whom wore veils, but he did recognize one who was the wife of a senator, and also a woman whose presence made him blush for shame. She was quite tall, with fair skin, blonde hair, and blue eyes. Marcus had seen her once in a brothel that he had visited near the Temple of Isis, in those sinful days before he had discovered the Lord Christ. He was so ashamed that he could barely concentrate on the Vigil service, when the lanterns were extinguished and the Easter Candle was lit in the darkness. The Lord's Resurrection was being proclaimed in a hymn composed of Greek and Latin words, and a little later the Hebrew Scriptures about Creation and the crossing of the Red Sea were being read by Atticus and a deacon named Quartus. But Marcus could not concentrate on them. When the people sang a hymn to the Lord Jesus, Marcus could barely sing, though Atticus had taught him the words; he kept thinking of that young woman to his right, who was totally unaware of him and singing quite cheerfully. She had a beautiful voice, and was pronouncing the Latin and Greek words with a German accent. "Lord Jesus, forgive my sin," Marcus said simply, again and again, to the point where he could once more pay attention to the service.

Now it was Bishop Telesphorus himself speaking, after he had proclaimed the narration of the Resurrection from Saint Mark's Gospel. His voice was clear, though with a bit of a rasp. *"For there are two ways,"* he was saying, *"that we may take while here on earth. One is the way to Life, which consists in believing in the Lord Christ the Son of God, who has redeemed us from our sins through his passion, death, and glorious resurrec-*

tion which we celebrate tonight. And this way to Life brings patience, charity, purity, and wisdom. It is filled with hope, and brings us a light and consolation that are beyond compare. But the road to death is filled with darkness and despair. By giving into pride and the sinful desires of the flesh, a man will be lost, and his life will end in the ultimate terror. He will not be able to come to the Light, that Light who is Christ, who is the victor over sin and death.

For our Lord said, "I am the Way, the Truth, and the Life," and "Do not be afraid, for I have overcome the world." He gives us a hope and a courage that the world cannot give. And that courage is shared not only by those who have faced torture and death, as so many saints have endured in this City, but also by those who love and serve Christ in their daily life. With great risk to themselves they spread his truth and message to those around them. And tonight we gather to welcome those men and women who have chosen the way to Life, who have completed their time of instruction, and have made their commitment to Christ the Lord of all peoples. They wish now to receive his saving Light and Grace through the sacred mysteries of Baptism, Confirmation, and the Holy Eucharist. We particularly rejoice for them and for their friends, as we now prepare for the great sacrament of Baptism.

After the homily, as the sacred mysteries were about to begin, Marcus and the other catechumens were escorted from the atrium. Marcus saw Numer standing behind Dédicus, and Scintilla behind Cynthia . . . their good friends and sponsors in Christ. He was extremely happy for them, as he left the room where the Eucharist was about to be celebrated, that joyful, ineffable sacrifice in which he could not yet participate, and in which Dédicus and Cynthia were participating for the first time.

As the service continued, the catechumens received instructions outside of the house; they were divided into three groups: one for men, one for women, one for children (both boys and girls together). The lessons were given by men and women disciples of Christ who had been following him for at least five years, and who had shown both consistent knowledge and practice of the Way. There were small fires in different parts of the field where the groups gathered, to the side and behind the house. As the instructor spoke, with a Gallic accent like that of Atticus, Marcus could hear the neighing of Justus's horses farther back in the field, mixed with the singing of the celebrants inside the atrium.

The instructor for the men's group, whose name was Vincentius, said nothing that Marcus had not heard before. For the past fifteen months, he had received a deep intellectual and practical training from Numer, Dédicus, and Atticus. But he still tried to listen carefully now to this speaker, who spoke of the importance of patience and charity in dealing with others, particularly with those in one's family and with close acquaintants. He gave the example of the widow's mite, in the Gospel, and how a little thing can do a great deal of good for spreading the kingdom of Christ. "For he who is faithful in a little thing, is faithful also in much," Vincentius said, quoting the Master. And then he gave real-life examples, which helped Marcus to think about his own life, especially in his home.

After the service was over, the entire group gathered in a garden area at the side of the house. There were lanterns and torches for illumination, and Marcus was able to meet Telesphorus. Numer introduced him as Marcus, the son of Gaius Metellus, Consul of Rome. "And brother of Junia," the bishop added as he took his hand. "Marcus," he said, with a faint smile on his lips, "I do pray for your father. He's a noble and honest man, and is doing much for Rome through his good work." Marcus nodded gratefully and bowed to him, but he couldn't think of anything particular to say except that Numer, Dédicus, and Atticus had helped him greatly in his life, and that he asked for the bishop's prayers. Then he stood in line to embrace Dédicus, who was clothed in a white garment, as were all the neophytes who had just received the sacraments. Dédicus was smiling very broadly and actually laughing—which he rarely did, for he had an intense and serious temperament. Marcus went up to him and embraced him warmly, as he would a brother. Dédicus told him excitedly, "I knew, when I tackled you on the street that day, that Christ would bring you to himself in some way, Marcus." And Marcus answered, "Please keep praying, Dédicus. I'm not there yet."

The women neophytes, in their own group, were laughing and talking excitedly among themselves, embracing and kissing one another. Marcus went closer to them and saw Cynthia. She looked very beautiful in her new white garment, and with torchlight sparkling brightly in her dark eyes, revealing her delicate cheeks and nose. He caught her glance, and waved at a distance to her. Then Cynthia smiled and waved back to him, as if to say: "I'm praying for you, Marcus, that you go all the way."

Before he left, Numer introduced Marcus to Justus and his family. Justus was a tall man with broad shoulders, his face deeply tanned from the many years he had worked on a farm in northern Latium. He greeted Marcus Roman-style, both men clasping each other's forearm. *He might be hard to beat in a wrestling match*, Marcus thought as he sized him up. As he began to speak with him, he discovered how Justus and his family had met his sister, and how they had witnessed her baptism in the catacombs two years earlier. "Your sister was wonderful," Constantia said. "She looked so joyful when she received the Lord Christ."

"And she knelt on the cold stone ground for so long," Timotheus added, with a big smile on his face, though it seemed the smile of one who had suffered. Little Carmina just looked up curiously at Marcus; she was playing a flute for the entertainment of the people, as she walked among the adults. But she remembered Junia most for the way she had picked up the apples for that man whose cart had turned over, on the way back to Rome on that first night.

XXVI.

Just a few weeks afterward, in late April, Quintus and Claudia married. The ceremony took place at the Temple of Juno, Claudia's choice. She loved the old Roman religion of gods and goddesses and, unlike many of her peers, had observed many of its prayers and ceremonies throughout her life. Quintus had no objection to the site of the marriage, though he no longer believed in the gods himself.

The Emperor himself, who was sick and ailing at his estate in Tivoli, sent a representative to the ceremony, wanting to show Quintus in this way the esteem that he had for him—not only for being the son of Cassianus, one of his leading generals, but also because he was the Prefect of his Guard. After carrying Claudia over the threshold of their new house, not far from Capitoline Hill, and spending only one night there, Quintus took her on their wedding trip to a resort town on the Adriatic Sea, facing the coast of Dalmatia. Quintus had served as a young army recruit there, and loved the scenery.

Cynthia attended the wedding ceremony at the Temple of Juno, but she was praying to the Lord Christ himself and to his mother—that Claudia and Quintus would have a very happy marriage, be faithful to one another, and be blessed with children. From what she could see, both of them already had those ideals, which were unusual for non-Christian couples those days in Rome. And she added a prayer for their conversion, so that someday they could be united in Christ's love and his Church.

Shortly before the wedding, she had asked Claudia for her freedom. At first, Claudia had been saddened by the request and, mentioning all the wedding preparations, had begun to object—but then, after many tears, and after Cynthia had offered to help her with all the preparations, she had consented. She recognized the good that Cynthia had done for her, and could not find it in her heart to refuse her anything.

She had earned her freedom. When Cynthia left, they agreed to keep seeing each other at least once a month, as they were now friends.

Cynthia was delighted to see that Marcus had become a catechumen, and she prayed for his entrance into the Church. But she was even more gladdened by a calling she had felt deep within her, which she had recently decided to pursue. After several months of thought and prayer, and with the encouragement of Scintilla and one of the priests who had instructed her, she had decided to give herself completely to Christ, as a virgin, for the rest of her life . . . just as Marcia and Scintilla had done.

Her choice had become more difficult after Claudia's wedding, because both Claudia and Quintus had told her that they could introduce her to several wealthy Roman men, any one of whom would be very pleased to marry her and make her the mistress of his household. Three of them had already spoken to Claudia about her.

But she was convinced that now only Jesus Christ could be her Lord and Master. He was truly the *Kurios*,* and she had found the greatest love with him, and in serving others for him. She could earn a living tutoring daughters of wealthy families in Rome, of whom she already knew many from her years in the households of Gaius and Publius. Her plan, as she had discussed with Scintilla and one of the priests, was to teach Christian slaves Latin and Greek in her free time, and help them to learn how to read and write, as she had done with Frieda. Because she had become so accomplished and articulate in the knowledge of the Faith, she had already been asked to instruct many of the inquirers and catechumens.

One of the first things she did, after receiving Claudia's good-bye embrace and moving to her new home, was to pay a visit to the catacomb where the bodies of Marcia and

* Greek: "the Divine Lord" (see 1 Corinthians 1: 2–3).

Junia were resting until the day of Christ's second coming. She had gone there often during her time as a catechumen, and after being baptized she had been there to the Eucharist with Father Atticus as the celebrant. On those occasions, she had prayed hard to both Marcia and Junia for her perseverance, and for Marcus. She had kept Marcia's letter with her, the one she had written to Junia years before, and which Junia had given to her in the prison cell—along with a scroll she had found in Junia's room shortly after her death. The scroll contained a passage from Saint Paul, and she read it often: "For you did not receive the spirit of slavery to fall back into fear, but you have received the spirit of sonship. When we cry, 'Abba! Father!' it is the Spirit himself bearing witness with our spirit that we are children of God." *

These words enchanted and thrilled her each time she read them, for now, with Christ and her complete dedication to him, she knew that she was truly free.

XXVII.

As he learned more about the Way of Christ, Marcus thought often of two other powerful expressions that Paul of Tarsus had written more than eighty years before: "*Caritas Christi urget nos*" and "*Veritatem facientes in caritate*." ** Truth was not something to be only learned or taught, but to be lived with charity and good works. Numer had insisted that creation is good in itself, and so are marriage and the home, contrary to what the Gnostics were teaching. Marcus therefore should try to find Christ and to bring him to those

* Romans 8: 15–16.

** The full texts are: "Speaking the truth in love, we are to grow up in every way into him who is the head, into Christ" (Ephesians 4: 15), and "For the love of Christ urges us on, because we are convinced that one has died for all; therefore all have died. And he died for all, that those who live might live no longer for themselves but for him who for their sake died and was raised" (2 Corinthians 5: 14–15).

around him. Vincentius's words about "little things" at the instruction of the Easter Vigil had also made a deep impact on him.

Coming home from classes, or later in the evening, he made a special effort to greet his mother with a kiss. At first she was quite surprised at this courtesy, but then she grew to expect it, and felt hurt if for some reason he neglected it. She was still a very fashionable woman, but she no longer spent hours in front of the mirror, or with exotic hairdressers. She had become more reflective and serious after her daughter's death. Marcus's changed attitude and actions reminded her of Junia's behavior in the last months of her life. But she could not bring herself to think that he was studying Christianity. It would be too much for her, or for her husband, to face; so she simply dismissed the suspicion from her mind.

Marcus also made the effort to interest himself in his father's career and work . . . something he had never done before, for he had simply considered him the income-gatherer for the family. Numer suggested that he go to some of his father's speeches or legislative sessions in the Senate. He forced himself to pay more attention to politics; and, if his father had had some meeting with the Emperor's assistants or with some governors from the provinces, he asked him questions. Gaius could not understand the change in his son's attitude, but he gave thanks to the family gods that at last he was coming down from the clouds of speculative philosophy, and seemed more interested in practical things. He even began to ask his opinions about various matters, especially what people were saying in the streets about him—for Marcus was constantly on the street.

As Father Atticus had urged him, he tried to find times for prayer each day. He began the day, just before sunrise, with a simple prayer of offering to Christ the Lord of the universe, and he also tried to spend time in meditative prayer before leaving for the Athenaeum. He liked to use the marble bench in the inner courtyard, which Junia liked so much, next to the pool. He knew that God was everywhere and was interested in the big and little things of his daily life. He tried to have a dialogue with him each day, asking his angel to deliver his prayer to heaven if he should get distracted or tired. He was especially moved to pray after reading passages from a scroll called *The Teachings of the Apostles*,* which Numer had given to him, and which spoke about the Way to Life in words very similar to what Bishop Telesphorus had used at the Easter Vigil Mass. Every day he read it, he desired more and more the day of his Baptism.

Having learned that the Christian should love his neighbor as himself, he tried to think of others more, and how he could help them. Often in the past, he had considered his father's *clientes* ** to be noisy fools who disturbed his sleep in the morning; but now, with the help of the Holy Spirit, he recognized that they too were human beings who had their needs, with families to support. One day, after his father had given the day's assignments to his *clientes*, Marcus noticed that Bombolinus was walking out with his face quite crestfallen.

He walked after him and said, "What's the matter, Bombo? Didn't my father have any work for you?"

Bombolinus was surprised that Marcus was even taking the time to speak with him—he had rarely done so before. But this time it seemed that he was in earnest. Not knowing what to think, he answered him simply. "No work, unfortunately, Master Marcus."

"And therefore," Marcus responded goodheartedly, "no fine dinner this afternoon, or conversations with praetors or senators?"

"No," Bombo answered uneasily, as if Marcus was not taking him seriously, or was making fun of him.

---

* The Greek name of this work is *Didache*, a document widely read in the second century, though it was not considered inspired.

** Political assistants.

"Well, let's you and me go to dinner today, and tomorrow I'll try to put in a good word with my father. He has to give an important speech in the Senate, and he may have some work for you."

Bombolinus could not believe it. Why would the son of Gaius take any interest in him? Who in Rome had ever heard of anyone doing a favor for another man and not expecting anything in return? When he returned home, filled with excitment at the prospect of having dinner and chatting with the son of a Consul of Rome, he told his wife, Flavia, about it. She could not believe it either at first. But then, after a moment or so, she narrowed her eyes and pointed her finger at her husband. "Be careful of him, Bombo," she said. "That's the sort of things that Christians do."

XXVIII.

Constantia was not the same after the stabbing of her son. In the last months of her pregnancy, she would have to lie down frequently, and she seemed more anxious about things. She began to bleed heavily, to the point that Justus made a special trip to Ostia and drove a physician he knew up to their home. After examining her, the doctor said that there was nothing he could do for her except to give her an herbal sedative. Justus consulted another doctor in Rome whom some friends recommended; he also had no cure, but he told Justus that if her sickness continued, he could perform an abortion for a minimum fee.

"We will never do that," Justus told him immediately. Then, drawing himself to his full height and looking down into the smaller man's eyes, he added, "And may God forgive you for what you just said."

In the meantime, Timotheus was recovering from the stab wounds he had received and could now do some household chores, though he was still quite weak. He and Carmina took on the things that their mother could no longer do, especially the cleaning and the cooking. If a quarrel began between them, they got over it quickly, so as not to grieve their mother. A source of great strength for the family was to pray and sing a hymn together every morning to Christ the Lord King, as the sun was rising. If Constantia was not well enough to leave her room, they would sing it there with her; and Carmina would always add a prayer aloud to the Virgin Mother of Jesus for her own mother and the baby. Many days also, she would bring her lyre to her mother's bedside, and sing the simple songs that she had composed. Her music comforted Constantia greatly.

For many days, Justus was not able to sleep with his wife. He made a mat of hay and put it on the floor in a corner of their room. One night, after making his wife as comfortable as possible, and after they said their night prayers together, concluding with the hymn of Simeon from Luke's Gospel, Consti told him with a deep yearning in her eyes, "I would so love for us to be together tonight, Justus, but it cannot be." Justus said that it was all right; he had prayed to his angel to strengthen him, as an angel had strengthened young Tobias in the Hebrew Scriptures and kept him pure for his young bride.

"How do you feel, Consti?" he asked as he held her hand gently.

"I fear we shall lose the child," she answered in a very tired voice. "But God will not lose her. She'll be part of his kingdom."

"She? How do you know that it is a girl?"

"I just know," Constantia answered him simply.

XXIX.

One week later, about the third hour of the day, Quintus was in his office, seated at the large table, its fine cedar legs supporting a white marble top. He was studying the Emperor's schedule for the weeks ahead. Though the Emperor was in his declining years, and spent much of his time in his luxurious estate in Tivoli, he occasionally traveled to Rome and other locations, and therefore required a large contingent of guards in his service. Quintus also had to review some reports on the protection of the frontiers in Britain and along the Danube; the Emperor was awaiting his opinion, along with that of other chosen officers of his army.

Quintus was interrupted in his thoughts by a quick rap at his door. It was assistant prefect Septimus. "Come in," Quintus said crisply, as he received his salute. He liked Septimus: hard working, always on time, with a cheerful attitude. It was rumored among some of the soldiers that he was a Christian, but Quintus had no problem with that. When he had seen Junia being led to her execution, he had been amazed at her coolness and courage, with a bravery in her attitude that matched the best of his soldiers before a battle. A few weeks earlier, one of the other assistant prefects had even presented a petition to him against Septimus, denouncing him as a Christian, but Quintus had refused to act on it.

"Sir," Septimus said, "requesting permission to take a two-hour leave to help a friend who lives just outside of the City, on the road to Ostia. I will need a chariot and two fast horses."

"Who is the friend, and why the rush?" Quintus asked.

Septimus hesitated for a moment, and could not get out the words. "It . . . it has to do with a family, sir, and a woman giving birth. She may lose the child. My friend needs to get there fast."

"A rather irregular request," Quintus observed, "for the use of a chariot in the Roman army. And possibly illegal. Is your friend a doctor?"

"Yes, sir, in a way of speaking."

Quintus shook his head doubtfully; he wanted to ask a few more questions but decided not to do so. He liked

Septimus, and he trusted him, knowing that he would never do anything that would disgrace the Roman army.

"Very well," he said, "permission granted. Take three hours if you need them. Ask Manius to give you two fast steeds for the journey, and if anyone asks you where you are going, just say 'by order of the Prefect.' Understood?"

"Yes, sir," Septimus answered. And as he saluted his commanding officer, he could not hide a grateful smile on his face. He left the office quickly.

Atticus was waiting for him just outside the large bronze door of the Praetorian Headquarters, which in those days had been temporarily shifted to the outskirts of Rome near the Aventine Hill. Justus had just informed him that Constantia was beginning to have contractions, and was about to deliver a baby. One of the disciples, a woman named Julia from the household of Gladion, had been with her for the last few days . . . but now they needed a priest urgently. Atticus immediately ran to the headquarters of the guard, which was not far from the Aventine House, and asked Septimus for help—knowing that he was an excellent charioteer, as well as a disciple of Christ. Septimus drove them swiftly through the streets of the City, as the people immediately made way for the imperial chariot. It seemed to Atticus that in only a few minutes they were on the road to Ostia. They made such good time that they quickly passed Justus in his fish cart. Justus had driven into Rome to give Atticus the message, and was then riding back as fast as he could to his home.

As they reached the front of Justus's house, Atticus jumped from the chariot and ran into the atrium. Timotheus was waiting for him at the door, and led him quickly to his mother's room. The child had already been born, a girl. She wasn't crying, as healthy babies do, but taking short breaths, struggling to stay alive. Julia was holding her, stroking her back, trying to help her to breathe, and singing a lullaby.

"Has she been baptized?" Atticus asked her immediately.

"Yes, Father, I did it right away, seeing that she could die at any moment."

"What is her name?"

"Maria Rosa."

Then Atticus, who had brought with him the sacred chrism that had been blessed by Bishop Telesphorus during Holy Week, gave her the sacrament of Confirmation. After asking God the Father to send the Holy Spirit, he dipped his right thumb in the chrism, and extending his hand over her he made the sign of the cross with it on the baby's tiny forehead, as he said: "Maria Rosa, be sealed with the gift of the Holy Spirit." And everyone present said, "Amen."

Then he asked Julia why she had named her Maria Rosa.

"Consti named her that. After she had given birth, I put the child on her lap and she said: 'Baptize her right away. Baptize her Maria Rosa, for she has such a pretty face, like a little red rose.' Then she fainted."

At that point, Justus burst into the room, and was able to see the little girl while she was still breathing. He took her into his strong arms and kissed her head and cheeks; then he gave her to Timotheus and to Carmina, who did the same.

"One more for his kingdom," Justus said to Atticus and Septimus. "God is good." Then he covered his eyes with his hands and began to weep.

XXX.

One day, a few months afterward, in October, Marcus approached the courtyard in front of the Domus Aventina. Numer was pacing up and down alongside the fountain, looking very serious, as was completely unlike him. When he saw Marcus, he did not deliver his usual short quip or joke, though he did give him a smile.

"What's wrong, Numer?" Marcus asked right away.

"We've just received word that the Bishop has been arrested. He has been denounced as a Christian by Envidius, chief priest of the Temple of Jupiter on the Capitoline Hill."

Marcus's quick mind began to work. "Could it be that Envidius was jealous because the cult of Jupiter has been declining in recent years, especially among younger people? Maybe he suspects that the Pope has been taking away his worshipers."

"Yes, I do think that's the cause," Numer replied. "Jealousy and ambition are behind most denunciations. There will be a trial, but it will only be *pro forma* and very brief. Though this Emperor has not been a persecutor of Christians, as Nero and Domitian were, the law is inflexible, and the sentencing will take place. It is very evident that Telesphorus is a Christian, and indeed is the leader of all the Christians in Rome. With all the Eucharists that he has celebrated in different places, with all the people he has known for the past eleven years[*]—the evidence is overwhelming. And Envidius has many spies."

"We need to pray," he added, and, taking Marcus by the hand, he turned his face to the eastern sky, toward Jerusalem, and led a short prayer to *Kurios*, the Lord Christ, and to Peter, his apostle and first bishop of Rome—asking that somehow, through a miracle, Telesphorus's life might be spared, for he was loved by all.

In the week afterward, during the bishop's imprisonment and trial, hundreds of Christian families throughout Rome were reciting the Second Psalm every day in their homes: "Why have the Gentiles raged and the people devised vain things? For the kings of the earth have risen, and the rulers have assembled together against the Lord, and his anointed one"—just as the Christians of Jerusalem had done when

[*] According to St. Irenaeus, Telesphorus was Pope in Rome between the years 125 and 136.

98

Peter was arrested there about a hundred years earlier—and *he* was released.*

But it was not to be. As Numer had predicted, the evidence against Telesphorus was overwhelming, and there were many witnesses. He was condemned to be chained to a cross, covered with pitch, and burned alive in the arena of the Colosseum. The entire Christian community was praying and suffering, but there was nothing they could do; it was the law of the Roman Empire. At the same time, when they heard the news, many of them were joyful, knowing that their bishop would soon be with Christ, and that he could intercede for them even more with the power of his suffering and prayers. None of them was surprised; sooner or later, martyrdom was the expected thing, especially for the Pope. It had been that way since Peter's arrest in Rome, seventy years earlier.

Telesphorus was kept in the Mammertine prison, under special custody, with a squad of twenty soldiers at the entrance. He was allowed two visitors a day, but none after sunset. The presbyters had arranged that one of these visitors would always be a priest, who would bring him Holy Communion. Atticus was chosen to bring him Communion twice in the two weeks of his imprisonment, a privilege that he would remember for the rest of his life. One of the presbyters was a Greek named Hyginus, who many thought could be the next Pope; he heard the condemned man's confession and prayed with him the day before his death.

The day of the execution was cloudy, and many thought that it must rain. As people lined up along the road to the Colosseum to view the procession of the condemned, they were complaining about the weather.

"Rain today would be no fun," one woman said.

"Just leave it to the Christians to spoil our celebration

* See Acts of the Apostles 4:26.

today. They're a bunch of boors, anyhow," chimed in the man standing next to her.

But someone else was thinking aloud. "Wait," he said. "What if it does rain and douses the fire that burns Telesphorus on the cross? Wouldn't that be a sign from their god that the Christians are right?"

A public holiday had been called for the event, and a program of spectacles had been planned at the Colosseum. After Telesphorus was executed, a woman who also had been condemned for being a Christian would be thrown to hungry lions. And after that there were to be several gladiatorial contests, featuring some net and lance fighters from Dalmatia who would be pitted against two famous Roman gladiators.

Marcus, Numer, and Dédicus were able to get a place in the front of the crowds lining the street, at a corner past which the condemned prisoners would be led. At first, Marcus did not want to along; from the time he was a small boy he hated violence, along with anything having to do with blood, fire, and the sword. He had gone to only one gladiatorial game in his life, and that was because one of his friends had dared him to go. He liked wrestling and horseback riding, but he preferred to keep apart from anything having to do with death or physical violence. It was out of friendship to Dédicus and loyalty to Bishop Telesphorus, who had anointed him as a catechumen and signed his forehead with the cross, that he had decided he should go.

The soldiers had put Telesphorus on a donkey, placing on his head a crown of thorns intertwined with laurel branches—similar to the wreath that emperors and conquering generals wore in their victory processions. It was meant here to be a mockery of the Christ, who had ridden on a donkey into Jerusalem while people proclaimed him as a king. There were also many graffiti on walls of buildings along the street showing a man on a cross with the head of a donkey. At certain intervals along the street going to the Colosseum, a few people were waving branches in front of Telesphorus, bowing and singing "Hosannah." The crowds were roaring with laughter; but Marcus, Dédicus, and Numer did not laugh. They were praying for Telesphorus and his perseverance.

Others in the crowd were hostile, shouting words of hatred against the Christians. Many were clenching their fists above their heads.

"So they caught the big fish at last . . . the atheist!"

"Filthy Christian!"

"Criminal . . . they should do the same to all of you!"

Telesphorus, his long brown beard mixed with gray, was nearly fifty years of age. His hands were tied in front of him, but he would now and again lift them and bless any people in the crowd whom he recognized as Christians. He smiled whenever he saw one whom he had recently baptized. When he passed by Dédicus, Marcus, and Numer, he blessed them and made the V-for-victory sign with the fingers of both hands. Farther down the street, Marcus saw Scintilla, Cynthia, and the young German woman who had been baptized with Cynthia. They looked as if they had been awake and crying the whole night; but when Telesphorus went by them, they had big smiles on their faces, and were actually cheering for him. Marcus was astounded that the women would dare to do that . . . they could be arrested. He, Dédicus, and Numer had said nothing when Telesphorus had blessed them, for fear of being discovered.

Behind the Pope was a woman seated in a chariot drawn by a single black horse, led by a soldier. Marcus immediately recognized her as a friend of his mother; he had met the woman at various social gatherings and parties. She had impressed him for her modesty and kindness. She was about forty years of age, and the wife of a very influential senator. From the red marks next to her eyes and alongside her mouth, it was evident that she had been beaten. Her hands also were tied, and, unlike Telesphorus, she did not look at the people along the streets but simply kept her head down, trying to pray.

Marcus turned to Dédicus and asked who had denounced her as a Christian.

"Her husband," the young Palestinian answered.

"Her husband? Why would a husband denounce his own wife?"

"I heard," Dédicus answered in a very hoarse voice, struggling with deep emotion, "I heard that the main reason was was that she would not agree to do an evil thing with him in their bedroom."

"And she's being thrown to the lions for that?" Marcus asked in a horrified voice.

"Yes," Numer joined in grimly. "Maybe the beasts now will be kinder to her than her husband was."

The whole scene was too much for Marcus. He was not mentally prepared for this. He felt his entire body begin to tremble. The shouts, the obscenities, the awful injustice of it all began to sicken him. He wanted to leave as soon as he could, after the condemned prisoners had passed by. The crowds were beginning to move on toward the Colosseum, and Marcus was hoping to go back to the Domus Aventina with Dédicus and Numer. But he was shocked to see that they had actually *joined* the crowds walking toward the Colosseum. And across the street, he could see Scintilla, Cynthia, and Frieda also going in that direction.

"What are you doing?" Marcus shouted to his companions. "How can you bear to see such an awful thing?"

Numer saw that Marcus was very upset, but answered him calmly.

"It's our way of giving glory to God right now, Marcus. They need our presence and our prayers. We must be close to them, as John was close to our Lord on the cross."

Marcus couldn't believe it. He could not agree. "But you can't go into the arena to be next to them, you'll be far away in the seats of the amphitheater . . . wait!" he shouted again. But it was too late; they had already disappeared into the huge crowd going to see the spectacle.

XXXI.

Marcus was shaken to the core of his soul. He understood now, for the first time fully, how dangerous was the path he had decided to take.

And to think that in six months he was to be baptized! He could be denounced at any time, and condemned to the arena like the man and woman he had just seen. Or, if somehow he could escape that, his career as a philosopher would certainly be ruined. Until this day he had learned to concentrate on the deep intellectual and good moral lessons of Christianity. He had made loyal friends. But he had been able to suppress from his mind the suffering, the mockery, the violence that went with being a Christian. He saw now the brutal, unforgiving danger of his situation—not only for himself, but for his father, who could lose his consulship if another child of his became a Christian.

He did not go straight back to his home, but returned by way of the park near Trajan's baths, where he had first made his decision to become a catechumen, and to break his engagement with Claudia. He tried to pray for strength to the Lord Christ, as Atticus had taught him to do, but he felt no consolation at all, only more fear and confusion. The little birds were flying once again from tree to tree, singing their mindless, cheery songs. Marcus looked up and, being alone, actually shouted at them, "Silly ones! Why can't you understand what I'm going through right now?" But then, he thought, hadn't Dédicus been silly that day in which he risked his life to save him from the chariot? Hadn't the Apostle been silly when he kept trying to convert the Jews, who would not listen to him? Hadn't Christ been supremely silly when he, the Eternal Logos and Son of the Father, had chosen to die on a cross? *And right now*, Marcus thought, *they're getting the pitch ready to cover Telesphorus for his cross . . . and the lions are being starved to devour that poor woman.*

Marcus couldn't think any more. His body was trembling, and his mind—usually so clear—was racing ahead with all kinds of strange thoughts. He walked over to the pond and looked at himself in the clear water. It was a cloudy day, and there was not enough light to see his face clearly, only a vague outline. "You are my son"—he remembered the words of the Second Psalm, which he had been praying all these days with Numer for Telesphorus's liberation. "This day I have begotten you."

But God had not heard their prayers, Telesphorus had been condemned to a terrible death, the mobs would have their entertainment, and he himself felt totally alone and on the edge of despair. *Lord, how can you permit this? Lord, in the middle of such pain and hopelessness, how can I be your son?*

With a very heavy heart he began to walk back to his father's house on the Esquiline. The streets were almost empty, many of the people having gone to the amphitheater. He walked through the courtyard of his house into the atrium, which had the bright red and gold fresco of the goddess Minerva that his mother had commissioned. "Minerva," he muttered, "the goddess of wisdom. Athena, sprung from Jupiter's brain! Should I pray to you now, and abandon Jesus Christ? It would certainly be much easier for me."

He wanted to go straight to his room and to lie down. He had slept very little the previous night, ceaselessly thinking about the executions that were to come in the morning, and overcome by the dread he had begun to feel. But as he approached his room at the end of the inner courtyard, he saw something that he had never seen before. His father, dressed in a simple white tunic, was standing at the door of Junia's room, sobbing. His whole body was shaking.

Marcus had never seen his father weep. It was against all of his dignity as a *paterfamilias*, as a Roman, and especially as a Stoic. It was not a manly thing to do, and he had always taught both of his children that tears were for the weak. Marcus had tried to live by those words, so that his surprise was now even greater: his father was both crying and trembling.

He walked up quietly behind him, and between his sobs he could hear him say, "You were such a brave girl, dear Junia, such a brave girl. And I wouldn't listen; I wouldn't listen . . . I struck you! Can you ever forgive me?"

Marcus didn't know what to do. He could go back to his room, and leave his father to his grieving. But he decided on another course of action. He came behind him quietly and touched his father's arm, to let him know that he was there. Gaius wheeled about suddenly, with a look of both anger and extreme embarrassment on his face. "Why aren't you at the Athenaeum?" he shouted at him with a fury arising from his embarrassment.

"They've closed it today, because of the execution of the Christians," his son answered.

"Oh, yes," Gaius said, trying to calm himself down, but still looking very chagrined. "I had forgotten." Then he turned once again and looked at his daughter's room, which he and Aurelia had kept just as it was during her life: the couch in the corner where she slept, the small night table with a looking glass and a large comb in front of it, the writing desk near the window to the courtyard.

"Father—" Marcus summoned all of his courage to speak. "Junia knows you loved her . . ."

"Yes," Gaius said softly, and without another word he crossed the courtyard to his study.

Marcus stood in silence for a moment where his father had stood, looking into his sister's room. He thought of how briefly she had been a Christian, only a month or so, and of how abrupt and shocking her death had been to them all.

He thought of his own efforts to persuade her to take the anti-Christian oath, and to manipulate her thoughts in taking it—but she had refused, saying that the oath would be a lie, and that Christ was her truest friend. Above all, his father's tearful words echoing in his own mind, he thought of her bravery.

For some reason his eyes fixed themselves on the small blue-and-red mosaic on the wall above Junia's bed. She had commissioned it to be made a few weeks after she had returned from the country villa to Rome, after Marcia's death. It portrayed a ship, sailing steadily ahead, toward a rising sun. She had never told anyone why she had chosen such a scene.

As he went to his room, Marcus reflected that at that very moment Telesphorus was probably being burned alive on the cross. When he reached his room, he didn't go to bed, but got on his knees and prayed for Telesphorus and for that poor Christian woman—that they would be strong until the end.

XXXII.

At the Athenaeum, the talk among the students was all about the events in the Colosseum the day before. Several remarked how courageous the Christians had been before their torturous deaths; neither the man nor the woman had shouted any kind of curses or protests, nor had they shown any kind of fear—but both had an attitude of prayer before they were killed. Telesphorus was looking to the sky when they were covering him with pitch, just before they set him afire. The woman was kneeling on the sand with her head down and hands folded as the three lions ran toward her. They had died in a very calm, almost joyful way. Many people were awe-struck at the sight.

When Marcus reached the Christian residence later, he learned that after Telesphorus and Fulvia had been killed, the amphitheater organizers let the Christians remove their remains from the arena grounds before the gladiatorial contests began. Numer and Titus were among those who assisted in the removal. When they reached the place of the burning cross, they found only a few charred bones and the skull of Telesphorus in a mound of ashes. They had knelt down reverently before them and gathered the bones into a copper box—engraved on top of it was the symbol of a fish . . . and beneath it "Telesphorus, Bishop of Rome," with the years when he had been Pope. They had then taken the box and buried it at a place on the Vaticanus Hill, very near Peter's monument, where there was to be a memorial prayer service the next day.

At the same time, a group of women had come into the arena with a shroud and had gathered the mauled remains of the woman who had been exposed to the lions. They and others took her body to one of the catacombs along the Via Appia, and there one of the priests had led a burial service for her; afterward they had sung a hymn to the Virgin Mother. The priest spoke to them of the great beauty of chastity, one of the ways in which Christianity brought light to the world.

Marcus noticed that the mood of the Aventine residence was very quiet that day. There was no joking around or laughter. No one looked particularly sad, either; but all made it a time of quiet acceptance and prayer. One fellow, Pyrrhus by name, whom Marcus did not know that well, told him there was more reason than ever to be joyful, because now they had two more intercessors in heaven.

Later that afternoon, Marcus found Atticus and told him about his fears of the day before and his strong temptation to quit his association with the Christians. He asked Atticus if he thought he should delay his baptism until his faith was stronger. But the priest told him not to worry, and said that temptation was part of God's plan to test people whom he had chosen to come to him. He said that all of them had known fear before embracing the Way to Life, and that the sacraments Marcus would receive would give him a great strength and confirm him in his fidelity.

XXXIII.

The new year came. As the weeks went by, Aurelia began to notice that her son was losing weight and seemed quieter than usual. After losing her daughter, she had grown far more attentive to her son; and she was also moved by his signs of greater affection toward her. But perhaps he had some illness? When she asked him, he replied that he was preparing for something very important in his life, and was fasting to be worthy of it. He would have liked to tell her that it was because of his coming baptism, but he could not do so.

"Son," she said apprehensively, "what is this very important event?" But as Marcus was about to answer, she put her hand over his mouth. She strongly suspected, with a mother's intuition, that he was preparing to become a Christian, but could not bear to hear him say it. Then, biting her lower lip nervously, she left the room.

In addition to his six weeks of fasting, Marcus was adding other prayers and sacrifices in order to gain fortitude and courage . . . he knew he still had softness and cowardice within him. Numer had given him a hair shirt* to wear for a time during two weeks of atonement for his sins; he wore it privately, under his tunic, upon his bare chest. He was praying often to the Lord Christ and to his guardian angel to help him be worthy. Two prayers that Dédicus had taught him were particularly useful. Both were to the Virgin Mother of Jesus: *Mater purissima, ora pro me; virgo sanctissima, adjuva me.*** He said these aspirations in moments of

* A rough, uncomfortable garment made of goat's hair from the province of Cilicia. It was worn as a means of personal mortification, and was similar to the sackcloth of biblical times.

** Trans.: "Mary, most pure, pray for me; most holy Virgin, help me."

fear and anxiety, and particularly in moments of impure thoughts and desires—when memories from the past would bother him. Ever since Junia's death, he had not sinned with a woman; and with the help of these aspirations, Marcus was also able to remain chaste with himself, for the first time in several years. This gave him a particular confidence and joy, as he looked forward to his entrance into the Church.

He also found great confidence in knowing that others were praying for him. Titus passed him one day on the Via Biberatica as Marcus was going to visit Dédicus in his apartment. Titus had introduced Dédicus to Christianity, and had first invited him to the Aventine. As he passed Marcus, he waved and gave him the V-for-victory sign with his hand, as Pope Telesphorus had done. When Marcus got to Dédicus's apartment, he told him about it.

"You know, Marcus," Dédicus said, "I never told you what I was thinking the day I tackled you in the street. I was thinking of a passage I had just read from the Gospel, where Christ said, 'Greater love than this, no man has than to lay down his life for his friend.' It was just then that I saw you in the middle of the street, about to be run over by the chariot. I didn't know you at all, but I just acted. But now God has given you to me as my best friend. Isn't it strange?"

Marcus could only smile in appreciation and gratitude, but then he joked. "You're right. It was a great way to become friends, and my ribs are still aching from it."

Others were asking Marcus for his prayers, also . . . he was soon going to be so close to Christ. One of the men who came occasionally to the Aventine, Silvius, was nearly forty years of age. He also spoke with Numer and Atticus regularly. Marcus had learned that Silvius worked at the same bank that was owned by Diodorus, Marcia's father. For years, he and Diodorus were the only Christians at the bank, and together they had been able to turn it into one of the more honest lending institutions in Rome. But now that Diodorus had died—more than three years ago—it had passed into the hands of one of Diodorus's other assistants, Aulus. This man was now juggling the figures of gains and losses at the bank in order to deceive the customers. Silvius was convinced that Aulus was using the bank's funds for his own private business, which had to do with the importing of olives from the eastern provinces. Silvius didn't know what to do, and asked for Marcus's prayers.

As the days approached for his reception into the Way of Christ, Marcus tried to reproduce in himself as much as possible the sentiments of Jesus. "Turn the other cheek. . . . Do good to those who hate you." For him, these were two of Christ's harder sayings, and Marcus examined his conscience about them. He had no enemies, as far as he could see, but he still felt hatred toward those who had destroyed his sister's life: toward Livia, toward her mother, Agrippina, and toward Antonius, her father. It was they who had hired the spy Culebros to stalk his sister, and who later had denounced her as a Christian. It was now more than two years since that had happened, but Marcus could not find it in his heart to forgive them.

This weakness of his bothered him, particularly because he was going to receive the Body and Blood of Jesus Christ very soon, and he wanted no trace of hatred in his soul. One day, he brought up the whole thing with Numer, who said that he should simply start praying for those who had hurt him.

"How should I pray such a prayer?" Marcus asked him.

"That all three of them find happiness—that someday they discover Jesus Christ, who is their savior . . . just as you have found him."

"It will be hard for me to do that," Marcus had answered him honestly, "but I'll try."

It was actually a little easier to do than he expected, partly because Livia's brother, Servianus, and he were becoming good friends. He had introduced him to Numer and had invited him to the Aventine house for a get-together with some of the other fellows. Servianus was a loyal—and perceptive—man, but his health was poor. Marcus learned from Servianus that Livia was very unhappy, suffering from anxiety and depression after Junia's death. She had a lively personality, and had recently married a wealthy Roman playboy in an extravagant ceremony on the isle of Capri; but already there was widespread gossip that her husband had taken a mistress. Though Livia wanted to have children, there seemed to be little chance that she ever would know motherhood—not only because of her poor health, but because her husband did not want children.

After hearing this, Marcus's heart was moved, and he made the effort to say a prayer each day for Livia; it occurred to him that he could even send her a grace by offering, for her, a certain boring philosophy class he was attending. It was harder for him to pray for Livia's mother and father. Antonius had sent the blackmail letter to his father after Junia had been discovered in the catacombs . . . Marcus asked the crucified Lord to give him a forgiving heart.

XXXIV.

Discalus and Gaius, also preparing for their baptism, were both receiving instructions from a priest who lived near the Forum Piscarium, and from Justus and Constantia—when her health was better. The sacraments of Christian initiation were to take place at Justus's house, as they had the previous year, celebrated by the new bishop of Rome, Hyginus, who had been elected Pope two weeks after the martyrdom of Telesphorus. Both Discalus and his son were very excited, for it was in that very home where they had both met Christ, through the words and example of Justus and his family.

Just a week before the Easter Vigil, in early April, Discalus and Gaius were sitting in their second-floor apartment in the tenement near Discalus's fish stand. They had just been fishing in the Tiber, between the two bridges, and had caught a huge pike. "Much better than what Justus brings us!" Discalus joked with his son as they were cooking it in their small oven. After supper, they sat together and were looking at a colorful bronze platter that Drusilla had liked, on which she used to serve them chicken stew and figs. They had not used the platter again after she died—they had found it unscorched by the fire that destroyed a whole floor of their tenement. Discalus and Gaius kept a fresh rose or garland on it, in remembrance of her; and tonight, Discalus had put a small lantern beside it.

"I think Mom would be very happy with our decision to become Christians, Dad," Gaius was saying.

"Really?" his father answered in a tone of surprise. "She never talked about them, as far as I can remember. How do you know?"

"Well," said the boy, "she and I spoke about them once in a while. I would ask her questions about the crazy things that I heard about them, and she always had something good to say about them. She thought they were honest people . . . with good families."

"I never knew that," Discalus said softly, with a certain wonder in his voice. "And why didn't she tell me?"

"Because . . ."—Gaius hesitated a minute, but then spoke out very quickly—"because she knew that you didn't like the Christians."

There was a moment of silence, as Discalus shifted uneasily on the wooden chair next to his bed, and thought about what his son had said. "How much I've changed, with God's help," he replied. And then he put his arm around his son's neck, and rubbed his cheek against his curly brown hair.

"Gaius, do you forgive me for all those times I hit you?"

"Of course, Dad." Gaius looked up at him with a mischievous grin on his face. "It didn't hurt that much."

And they both began to laugh.

THE FINDING OF LOVE

XXXV.

The Easter Vigil came at last in the first week of April. For Discalus and Gaius, it was the happiest moment of their lives. As they had received instructions in the Faith, they had grown closer, and they had met a group of people who gave each of them a greater purpose and joy in their lives.

Marcus asked permission to be baptized on the same evening in the catacomb where his sister was baptized and buried. At first he was hesitant to ask for such an exception for himself; but he had prayed about it, and saw clearly how much his sister had helped him in his journey to Christ, even after she had died. He also knew that the sacraments he was about to receive would unite him to the whole Christian community that evening, especially the sacrifice of the Lord's Body and Blood . . . which he was yearning to receive.

Father Atticus was to perform the ceremony. Numer and Dédicus also were there, along with several others who lived at the Aventine. Three of them had volunteered to survey and patrol the road and trees outside of the catacomb, both before and after the ceremony, to make sure that there were no spies in the area. All knew how Junia was betrayed, and they did not want the same thing to happen to her brother.

For Marcus, it was the greatest moment of his life. He had never visited the catacomb where his sister had been received into the Church; he now asked, before the service was to begin, to visit Junia's grave. Atticus, who knew exactly where it was, as he had conducted two prayer services there on the anniversaries of her death, showed him the way through the dark winding passages of the catacomb. They came to an alcove at the end of one of the passages, and Atticus handed Marcus the oil-fed lantern, pointing to a slab of marble toward the bottom of the wall. After some coaching from Atticus, Marcus found the face of the tomb of Marcia first . . . carved with the same image that Junia had seen almost four years before, a ship on the waves, and underneath it an inscription in Greek: YOUR SHIP HAS COME. SAIL ON, MARCIA, SAIL ON. Marcus then knew why Junia had put that bright mosaic in her room. And suddenly, as if for the first time, he understood how much Marcia, that funny Corinthian girl with the red hair, had meant to his sister— just as Dédicus, Numer, and Atticus had meant so much to him.

He then passed the lantern's light to the left of Marcia's tomb, to the grave beside it. There too he saw the image of a sailing ship, similar in form, but the words beneath it were different. They said: DANCE, JUNIA, DANCE FOREVER. Marcus was puzzled, and looked up at Atticus, who was standing directly behind him. "Can you explain these inscriptions?" he asked.

"Just after Junia was beheaded, our sisters went to gather her remains in a shroud, and brought her here to bury her. As you know, your father acted nobly in allowing her remains to be buried by Christians, because she was of our Faith. They decided to place her next to her best friend, and after a few months they also etched a sailing ship on her tomb; they were about to put the same words as on Marcia's tomb when Scintilla asked them to put words about dancing—because Cynthia had told her about Junia's last words. When she left the prison cell at the Colosseum, she had said: "Now I shall really dance, Cynthia, dance forever.""

Marcus put the lantern once again close to his sister's resting place, and then it came to him. Yes, Junia had always loved to dance. When she was little, she was always asking her big brother to dance with her. After she had met Marcia, she had learned some new steps, and seemed to find a special energy and joy in dancing even if she was alone. He remembered that she had done a mysterious little dance in her room that day when he was trying to convince her to offer incense to the statue of the Emperor.

He knelt there with his hands folded for a few minutes, looking at the inscription. He could only give thanks to the Holy Spirit for this extra gift on the night of his baptism. As Marcus rose to his feet, Atticus pointed out a nearby fresco of the Good Shepherd . . . just as Scintilla had pointed it out to Junia when she first came to the catacomb. The confident, smiling face of a young shepherd, with a lamb held firmly on his shoulders. And Marcus knew that, just as Christ the Good Shepherd had sustained Junia in all her sufferings, he had given him the perseverance to reach this important moment of his own life. He thanked God for his merciful providence. And he also thanked his sister for all that she had done for him. It was clear to him now—tears were filling his eyes—that she had never left him during the past three years; she had been with him in all of his wanderings and doubts, interceding before God for him, and was with him here too, as he was about to enter the Church.

Numer and Dédicus had joined them, after lighting the candles and preparing the altar for the Eucharist in the front part of the catacomb, near the entrance.

"My friends," Marcus said in a broken voice, "I'm just learning, once again, what a wonderful sister I had."

"Ah," Numer answered him warmly, "what a wonderful sister you *have*."

And as they led him back to the more open part of the catacomb—where his other friends from the Aventine were waiting, and where the baptismal water, the holy Chrism, and the bread and wine were all prepared—Marcus was sure that he had found Christ at last. In a very short time, now, all his sins would be washed away, and he would be made truly a son of God.

XXXVI.

In the weeks following Marcus's Baptism, Numer spoke often with him about his friend Justin, who was still in Ephesus. He believed that Justin could help the Christians of Rome . . . to strengthen their faith, and to give them confidence in dealing with their peers, especially in the schools, where most teachers were against them.

Marcus knew what Numer meant. In his classes at the Athenaeum, his professors went out of their way to ridicule Christianity and its ideas. According to them, Christians were superstitious, ignorant people who were very stubborn in their beliefs. It was the same kind of thinking that Marcus himself had had before he studied and understood Christianity's teaching. In his classes, when his teachers poked fun at Christ, he was annoyed; but he lacked the philosophical vocabulary to speak up and defend Christianity. He was afraid of going too far in his objections to the lecturers . . . lest he himself be identified as a Christian or ridiculed by his peers. So he limited himself to asking a dissenting question.

"We need to have a thriving philosophical and theological school here," Numer insisted with both Marcus and Dédicus. "We need to form philosophers who are both good philosophers and good Christians, and to show people that faith and reason have the same source, and lead in the same direction. That is exactly what Justin can do with his insights and experience. What is more, I have seen signs that Gnostic errors are spreading from the East into Rome.* There are certain teachers right now who are presenting Christ as a subordinate being, not really divine, who is only one among a world of inferior beings emanating from God. Such an idea is very insidious, and it could undermine the Church in Rome."

* The heretic Marcion arrived in Rome about A.D. 140 and proceeded to form his own school of Gnosticism, which taught that matter was evil and that the God of the Old Testament was evil. He went on to form a separate church, which deceived many of the faithful. He was excommunicated in 144.

Both Marcus and Dédicus agreed that Numer was right. Justin already had a following in Ephesus, thanks to his brilliant lectures and his book *Dialogue with Tryphon*, which showed in a masterful way that Jesus Christ was truly the Messiah announced by the Hebrew Scriptures. Marcus was particularly interested in Justin's view of the Logos, and how that Logos was prefigured and present in an incomplete way in the philosophers he was studying. He was hoping that he could be of service to Justin, in order to propagate his ideas.

The three of them set no date for their trip to the East, for as the situation in Rome then seemed relatively serene, they let time go by. Meanwhile, Marcus and Servianus had become good friends. Servianus too was impressed with the notion that the meaning and message of the Christian Logos, the Word through whom all things were made, could have been embedded in the great minds of the past. He also had a generous and loyal character; Marcus felt so at ease with him that he told him that he was a Christian, and then introduced him to Numer and Dédicus.

On holidays, Marcus invited Servianus to go horseback riding with him. They would have races in some fields outside of the City. These Servianus, who was as good a horseman as Marcus, invariably won. Marcus teased him about that, because Servianus was lighter and had the advantage. "Next time," he told Servianus, "in order to make the race even, we shall put a twenty-pound weight on your horse, and then yourself."

One day, after they had been riding for a while, Servianus motioned for Marcus to dismount. They were in a remote field, at the edge of some woods. An old log on the ground served as a bench, as Servianus—in a serious mood—and Marcus sat and rested. Before speaking, Servianus examined the woods behind them, to make sure that they were alone.

"Marcus," he said, his large brown eyes fixed on him, "I have two things to tell you, one good and one very bad."

"Start with the good thing," Marcus said.

"The good thing is that I thank you for the prayers you've made to your god for my sister, Livia. She seems to be in better spirits, despite her disastrous marriage, and she is happy for her friend Claudia and her marriage to Quintus. She was jealous of her at first, because she once had her heart set on Quintus; but Claudia is such a good friend of hers that she has forgotten her envy. Claudia is helping her to be much more calm about things."

Marcus smiled and said, "I'm truly happy for her. But tell me now, what is the bad thing?"

"It's about my father and mother. . . .and you."

"Me? What do I have to do with your father and mother?"

"You're in real danger, Marcus; they're plotting against you. It's pretty well known by now in Rome's high society that if you're not a Christian, you certainly have Christian sympathies and many Christian friends. You've been seen with them often."

Marcus shifted uncomfortably, looking at the ground. "Yes," he said, "I suppose that is obvious by now."

"Well," Servianus continued, "you probably also know that my father has never liked your father and continues to eye the consulship for himself. But your father has a sterling record and an impeccable career in the Senate, so the only way he can undermine him is . . . through blackmail."

"That's what he did with my sister." Marcus said in a low voice, trying to resist the bitter feelings welling up in his breast. Despite all of his efforts to be a Christian, those feelings were still there.

"Yes," Servianus said, as he grasped Marcus's arm warmly. "But please brace yourself for this. Now he is thinking that if he could prove that you also are a Christian, he could destroy Gaius's career permanently. Two children who have joined the Christians! He is still amazed that even after Junia's condemnation, your father was named Consul; but he thinks that that could never happen again."

"He's right," Marcus answered him honestly.

"To get to the main point, Marcus: My mother and he are going to hire a spy to watch your every move in the City. And he will be a citizen, not a slave like Culebros, who spied on Junia . . . so that he can testify against you in court. Marcus, my friend, your life is in danger, and so is your father's career. I think the best thing you can do is to leave Rome, and soon."

Marcus stood up quickly and scratched his head nervously. It was a fairly chilly day, and a wind was blowing; he adjusted his riding cape.

"It had to come, Servianus; it had to come. Sooner or later, I knew it would come. I've been lucky so far, my angel and my sister have been protecting me."

"Your angel?" Servianus asked with a raised eyebrow. "You'll have to tell me someday what you Christians mean by that . . . Is it something like a protecting spirit, like the gods of the hearth?"

"Yes, it's something like that," Marcus replied. "And, Servianus," he added as he gripped his arm with his own, "you're a true friend, as good a friend as I'll ever have. I will pray for you more now to my Lord Jesus Christ, so that someday you can join us."

The next day, Marcus told Numer about his conversation with Livia's brother, and after checking with Dédicus, they agreed immediately to go to Ephesus—the three of them. It was the best time to leave Rome: the sooner, the better.

XXXVII.

Gaius was not surprised when Marcus told him of his plans for a trip to the East. They had discussed this possibility almost two years before, connected with the new "philosophical system" that Marcus had been studying. Now Gaius was more open to letting his son do his own will—not only because Marcus was of majority age, but also because

Marcus's entire attitude toward him and Aurelia had greatly improved. Gaius could not explain the improvement. Perhaps it was an effect of the new philosophy that his son was studying: he was not so absorbed in his books, he had moderated his temper, he cared more about them. But he did remind Marcus, before he left, that he would be expected to consider marriage with the woman chosen for him . . . though he would not be forced . . .

Aurelia was more apprehensive about her son's journey. Of course, she was very moved by Marcus's increased kindness and thoughtfulness, but still she was nervous, having noted the same change in her daughter during the last year of her life. And when Marcus once introduced Numer and Dédicus to his parents, her suspicions grew. One of her friends had spoken to her recently about a group of young men who were Christians, and about a philosophy teacher who was their leader. Now she learned that Marcus planned to travel with those same two young men to Alexandria and Ephesus . . .

When it came time for Marcus to leave, she could not contain her anxieties. She was very direct with him.

"Son," she said, as he was putting his books and clothing into a large travel bag, "I want you to be honest with me."

Marcus stopped packing, and looked at her directly, with a smile.

"Marcus," she repeated, "tell me truly, as you are my son and I am your mother: Have you become a Christian?"

Marcus, like his sister, hated any type of deceit. With a look of helplessness in his eyes, he said, "Yes, Mother, I have been a Christian for several weeks now."

Aurelia looked away from him, and began to groan to herself. She covered her face with her hands, and shook her head. But her son immediately took her hands and kissed them.

"Mother, please understand. I did what I had to do in order to find the truth and a real purpose to my life. It's a long and complicated story. But I have found great happiness in following Jesus Christ, and I pray that you and Father will one day share it."

"It's so dangerous, Marcus, and so . . . unpopular. You know that my good friend Fulvia was killed last year for being a Christian; she was one of the finest people I ever knew. Oh, Marcus," and here she raised her voice piteously, "are they going to kill you too?"

He took hold of his mother's arms and looked at her light blue eyes, now filled with tears. "Don't worry, Mother. I'm going away for a little while now. Things will be safer that way for me." He resolved not to tell her of Antonius's plot to hire a spy . . .

His plan seemed to console her somewhat, but she added, as if to encourage him to rethink what he had done: "You know that your father has placed high hopes in you, Marcus. He hopes that someday you will be a lawyer or a statesman, and he's also thinking of a young woman for you to marry when you return."

Marcus could only say: "I know that Father has high hopes in me, Mother. But please understand that I also must do what I must do. I have found something wonderful, and I hope that someday, through some miracle, you and he will find the same thing."

Aurelia dried her eyes. "It must be so, then, Son. But I will pray to the goddess Minerva for you to reconsider your decision." Then she set her face hard, adding, "And I will not say anything of this to your father; that you must do yourself, on the day that you choose."

Marcus saw then how much his mother had changed. There was a depth and a calm about her now, which he greatly admired, and which he had seen developing in her over the past two years. "*Vale, mater carissima, vale*" (Good-bye, dearest mother, good-bye), he said, as they gave each other a warm embrace, and Aurelia kissed her son on both cheeks.

XXXVIII.

The ship to Alexandria was docked at Puteoli.* It was a large sailing ship, which had just delivered a load of grain for Rome, and which was now loading some three hundred passengers to take to the eastern provinces; on its wooden bow was a large ornate carving of the twin gods Castor and Pollux, protectors of sailors. The sailing season was in full swing; it was the end of June.

As Marcus looked to the shore from the deck, he thought once again of his father . . . yes, Gaius Metellus Cimber, of the illustrious line of Scipio Africanus, the conqueror of Hannibal himself at the famous Battle of Zama more than three hundred years before. Gaius, a man loyal to Caesar and to all the laws of the Roman state. How could he ever tell such a father—not only of his decision to become a Christian, but of his desire to remain unmarried for the rest of his life? The heart of Gaius Metellus Cimber, who so wanted to continue the family name, would be broken. First, to lose a daughter whom he had loved so much, and now to lose a son, in whom he had put new hopes—as his mother had told him . . .

Marcus shifted his stance uneasily as he leaned over the rail and studied the motion of the water beneath as the ship slowly slipped away from the dock. Would his father actually harm himself, as some Stoics had harmed themselves when they considered their lives meaningless or were under severe constraint? It was a horrible thought. No, he muttered to himself, as he clenched his fists. The God whom he was preparing to serve now with all of his body and soul would never permit it! There would be a way, somehow, for his father to accept his son's decision. The apostle Paul's brave words ran through his mind: "For those who love God, all things work together for good." **

* A large seaport used by the Romans, near present-day Naples.
** See Romans 8:28.

He resolved to stop thinking, or worrying, about his decision. The important thing was to pray hard, and to entrust the whole situation to the Lord Christ himself, to his Mother Mary, and to his sister.

EPILOGUE

Bombolinus was sorry to hear that Marcus was leaving. He remembered that fine dinner he once had with him, and how the young man had been true to his promise . . . he had put in a good word for him with his father. Gaius gave Bombolinus an assignment on the Senate floor the very next day, and had even let him address the senators for two minutes by himself——by way of introduction to Gaius's topic. It was one of Bombolinus's finer moments, and he boasted about it to all of his friends. And Marcus, before he left, had greeted him kindly several times and done him other favors.

The morning after Marcus left Rome, as Bombolinus made his way to the estate of Consul Gaius on the Esquiline Hill, he passed a number of other Romans like himself, going to greet their patrons, and he found himself thinking in a way he had never thought before. *Why couldn't I do a favor for one of them, without expecting anything in return?* Even if this was something that only Christians did, as his wife had warned! He thought of his colleague Timon. His wife had just had a child, and he was not doing so well in the Consul's plans. Perhaps he could put in a good word to the Consul for him today, or give him a share in an assignment he had just received . . .

Later in the day, at the other end of the City, on the Via Biberatica, Discalus sat on a wooden stool beside his fish stand, watching the crowds passing by. It had been a fairly poor day for sales, but he knew the reason. People were going to see the gladiatorial shows, which today featured a contest between two famous Macedonian fighters and two net- and spear-throwers from Numidia. For more than two years now he not gone to any of the games, though he could hear the frenzied roar of the crowds from his shop. Those of the Way did not go to such public spectacles, when men's blood was being shed for mere entertainment.

He looked up and saw a common sight: An elderly lady in a light purple palla came down the street, went up to the *lares* shrine,* and cast in a few bits of incense. Before, Discalus had looked with indifference at this woman and the repeating scene. But now, as she said her prayers, Discalus was praying for her to Christ the Savior, that somehow, someday, she would discover that *he* was the true protector of Rome . . . not the street gods.

The sun was just reaching its zenith, and it was time for the Syrian to pay his visit. "Fishmonger!"—he heard that loud taunting voice again, as he had so many times before, the voice of Bullio, a large Syrian servant from Gladion's household, with silver rings dangling from his ears. "Once again," Bullio quipped, "I must lower myself to give you some business."

The same anger and bitterness rose up in Discalus's mind as he had felt so often before when he had been abused by this man. In earlier years, he would have uttered some curses under his breath; but now, as a Christian, he decided it was time to do something different. Slowly rising from the stool, he looked up at the big man who had so often ridiculed him.

"Bullio," he told him resolutely, "you don't have to buy fish here if you don't want to. I am a Roman citizen; you are not. My father fought under Trajan, and I pay a tax to the City treasury on everything I sell. It's true that my business is small, and I'm well aware that your master could probably ruin me tomorrow if he wished, or buy me out. But I ask you, as one man to another, to treat me and my business with respect. If you will not, please leave right now."

Bullio looked very confused for a moment, as if he had just heard something impossible. He looked down at his big

* A small stone shrine honoring the protecting gods of the City.

125

feet, embarassment on his face. After a moment he turned his eyes back to Discalus, and said in soft voice that he was sorry, and could he please have five mackerel and two mullets. Discalus nodded, placed the fish carefully into Bullio's basket, and put a protective cloth on top of them. As Bullio reached into his pocket for the denarii to pay for them, Discalus caught his arm. "It's all right," Discalus said, "A gift from Discalus's shop to your master Gladion, for all the good business that he has given me over the years."

The Syrian looked at him, once again speechlessly, and then uttered something like "Thank you." He walked back toward his household on the Quirinal Hill, shaking his head, trying to understand where Discalus had suddenly gotten such courage.

After he had left, Discalus glanced toward the back of the shop; Gaius was copying some verses from The Aeneid on a wax tablet. He was to memorize twenty verses and recite them in school tomorrow. The boy already knew the good news about Silvia; he was to have a new mother, and Discalus hoped that Gaius would love her as he had loved his mother, Drusilla. The child already liked Silvia, not only for her good cooking, but for her sense of humor. Best of all, she was a new Christian like them; Discalus had met her when they were both learning the Faith together as catechumens.

There were no customers in sight, so Discalus walked down the street toward the *lares* monument. As he did so, he said a prayer to his angel for Septimus the winekeeper, a good friend of his. He had already spoken to him a little about Christ, and wanted to introduce him soon to Justus and his family . . . and to Photius, a baker who had just set up a shop down the street, and who also was a Christian. He planned to invite all of them to his wedding with Silvia, which was coming very soon.

As he neared the *lares* monument, his eyes fell on the small plot of sand below it. Someone had stomped out the outline of a fish he had traced there earlier that morning. He went back to the shop and borrowed Gaius's stylus. Returning to the monument, he traced the outline of a fish on the sand once again, but this time he added some letters underneath it: ICTHUS, the Greek word for fish, but whose letters signified JESUS CHRIST SON OF GOD SAVIOR.